BOTANICAL
FOLK
TALES

OF
BRITAIN
AND
IRELAND

BOTANICAL
FOLK
TALES

OF

BRITAIN

AND

IRELAND

LISA
SCHNEIDAU

For my mother, Pamela Jean Schneidau
and my grandmother, Florence Annie Stratton
with love

Cover illustrations: © David Wyatt

First published 2018
Reprinted 2019 (twice), 2020

The History Press
97 St George's Place,
Cheltenham, GL50 3QB
www.thehistorypress.co.uk

British Library Cataloguing in Publication Data.
A catalogue record for this book is available from the British Library.

ISBN 978 0 7509 8121 7

Typesetting and origination by The History Press
Printed and bound by Imak, Turkey

CONTENTS

About the Author	8
Acknowledgements	9
Introduction	11
1 Asleep in the Dark	15
The Forest of the Yew	17
The Apple Tree Man	18
The Travelling Tree	23
Mossycoat	25
2 The Quickening	37
Bride and the Cailleach	37
Crooker	42
The Fairy Widower	47
The Basketmaker's Donkey	51
Maon and the Willow	52
3 Struggle and Hope	58
The Green Mist	59
Goblin Combe	63
The Blackthorn Tree	65
Betty Stogs and the Fairies	67
No Man's Land	70

4	Joy and Sunshine	72
	The Fairy Shawl	73
	Yallery Brown	78
	The Field	85
	The Tulip Pixies	90

5	The Height of the Green	95
	The Juniper Tree	96
	The Legend of Knockgrafton	97
	Jack and the Beanstalk	103
	The Hornbeam Tree	119

6	Ripening Time	122
	That's Enough to Go On With	123
	The Last of the Picts	127
	Tom Fitzpatrick and the Leprechaun	129
	The Fine Field of Flax	133
	The Curse of Pantannas	136

7	Harvest and Home	145
	Lazy Lawrence	146
	The Crows and the Pear Trees	148
	The Farmer and the Boggart	150
	Harvest Daftness	154
	Two Moons in May	155
	Kate Crackernuts	161

8	The Turning of the Wheel	167
	The Elder-Tree Witch	168
	The Wonderful Wood	171
	Judge Popham's Oak	172

The Spectre Bridegroom   175
Donald and the Witches   179

Story Sources and Further Reading   183

ABOUT THE AUTHOR

Lisa Schneidau trained as an ecologist. She has worked with wildlife charities all over Britain to restore nature in the landscape, in roles including farm advisor, river surveyor, political lobbyist and conservation director. Lisa is also a professional storyteller, sharing tales that inspire, provoke curiosity and build stronger connections between people and nature. She lives on Dartmoor.

Acknowledgements

Where possible, I have drawn on multiple sources for every traditional story retold in this book. My huge thanks to all the folklorists, botanists and authors whose work has influenced and informed the stories. I have provided a full list of references and sources, but I'm particularly grateful to Katherine Briggs, Richard Mabey, Jacqueline Memory Paterson, Niall Mac Coitir, Ruth Tongue and Roy Vickery. Thank you to Halsway Manor Library and the Ruth Tongue Archive for allowing me to interpret some of the lesser-known folklore that Ruth collected. My thanks also go to all the storytellers who have collected and shared these tales in the telling, and upheld the oral storytelling tradition through the generations. I hope that I have honoured their stories well here, and added something useful to the tradition.

Thank you to the storytelling community – they have been very generous in their support of this project and in pointing me towards story sources. Particular thanks to Michael Dacre, Nick Hennessey, Sharon Jacksties, Lisa Kenwright, Clive Pig, Jess Wilson, and to Shonaleigh Cumbers and Simon Heywood, who suggested I write this book in the first place. Many story audiences and school groups have listened and shared my stories during the last few years and given feedback and ideas, and they have helped to shape the content of this book.

Thank you to David Wyatt for his stunning cover artwork, and to everyone at The History Press for their support and advice in bringing the book together.

I'm grateful to Ronnie Conboy, Moira Houghton, Karl Schneidau, Beccy Swaine and Jo Swift for proofreading and comments on the text. My father Oscar Schneidau, my brother Karl, and my family and friends have provided amazing support and encouragement throughout the project.

Introduction

I was lucky. I was a little girl growing up in 1970s Buckinghamshire with a mother and a grandmother who loved wild plants, and six fields of ridge-and-furrow, green-winged orchid meadow behind our house.

I remember when the moon daisies were nearly as tall as me, when we picked field mushrooms from the fairy rings and fried them for breakfast, when I could run through the middle of ancient hawthorn hedgerows and travel by the secret ways down to the magic old willow tree over the pond. I remember the carpets of cowslips, the endless blue butterflies, the quivering quaking grass, and the blackberries in autumn.

When we weren't exploring the fields, we were out looking for orchids on Ivinghoe Beacon, plant-spotting along the canal towpath of the Grand Union Canal, picking sloes on Dorcas Lane, collecting conkers at Mentmore or kicking the prickly sweet chestnuts around at Woburn. I inherited an insatiable curiosity for plants of all kinds and, with a vivid imagination as always, I wanted to know the stories: why? what? how does it feel to be a green living plant, a meadowsweet compared to a bee orchid?

Some time around 1980, the local farmer attacked our beloved fields. In the space of a week, the hedgerows had been razed, the land drained and the grassland ploughed up. Our willow tree house was cut down. One single crop of carrots was grown in the heavy Thames clay and then the land was left for fallow. In a single act of mindless vandalism, following the farming policies of the time, our wildflower paradise was gone. I can still feel the knot of deep grief that twisted in our bellies that year. We'd never heard of nature conservation, which was still in its infancy at that time.

Two science degrees, many years of working for wildlife trusts all over Britain, and many conservation projects later, storytelling found me. I was intrigued by the tradition: the richness of the stories, the skill and generosity of the tellers. Here were ancient tales that had been good enough to be passed down the generations, that might hold some of the old ways and the old wisdom. Storytelling caught my imagination and I started to try it myself.

I watched the storytellers at nature reserve events. They were telling stories of Coyote from America and Anansi from Africa. They were great stories, but they came from thousands of miles away; they had little to do with the nature and landscape that we were in. Where were the stories of this landscape, the things that grow and live and die here, the traditions of our own wildlife? And could those stories help us, living in Britain and Ireland, to reconnect to our own fragmented ecology?

This book is the first result of my search to answer those questions.

Here are thirty-nine folk tales about plants from Britain and Ireland. I have chosen this geography because plants don't respect political borders, and because of the ways in which the cultures of our countries share a common heritage. Although there is a wealth of plant folklore in these islands, actual folk tales with plants as a main feature are more occasional. They include stories about wildflowers, trees, and plants used for food, fibres and other human uses. I have chosen the stories that I particularly like and that I feel resonate with our natural history and our heritage.

These are my own versions of traditional tales. I have hunted out stories from many different sources: folklore archives and collections, natural history literature, and of course listening to storytellers. Some tales are well known, others more obscure. Like all storytellers, I am grateful to those who have collected and told these stories all down the generations, known and unknown. I have tried wherever possible to pursue a story back to its oldest referenced source. A list of story sources and further reading is provided.

The stories are presented according to the wheel of the year, starting when the sun is at its lowest at the winter solstice and continuing through the seasons and the old festivals. This is a very natural way to work with our stories about plants, even better if they are being told outside in the wild. Often the stories contain magical beings such as fairies, giants and pixies. I will leave it up to you to decide how much these characters represent the interface between humans and nature – the magic of life where nature cannot speak for itself – and how much they might be real!

I have told many of these stories to different audiences, indoors and out in the field, sharing ideas and emotions that the stories provoke. This book has been written as a resource to be used for storytelling; so, even better than reading the stories, do tell them to others. That is the way that stories change, and grow, and stay alive year on year. They are stories for all ages, although some are darker than others, and the teller will need to decide which stories to share with very young ones.

I hope you have as much fun reading and telling these stories as I have had in discovering them.

1

Asleep in the Dark

Have a mouth of ivy and a heart of holly.

Ireland

We start at midwinter, when most plant life is dormant. This is a time of the longest darkness. The winter guardian plants – bruised ivy, spiky holly and the yew with its vibrant red yew-gogs – give us some hope and cheer during the dark times. We can celebrate the turning of the year and the return of the sun, but there is still a long way to go, and there's little to sustain people or beasts in the meantime. Yet tiny sparks of plant life are everywhere, if you look. The wheel of the year doesn't stay still.

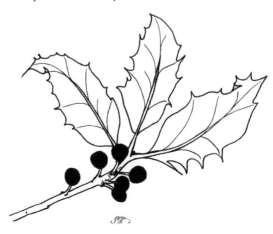

THE FOREST OF THE YEW

Yew trees remind us of everlasting life in the dark times of the year. The oldest yew trees in Britain are estimated to be over five thousand years old. Yews protect our churchyards and they are often associated with the dead and the Otherworld.

The Tylwyth Teg *are the Welsh fairy people, corresponding to the* sidhe *in Ireland and the fairy folk in England and Scotland. This story comes from Powys.*

In a place called Mathavarn, in Llanwrin, there was a wood called *Ffridd yr Ywen*, the Forest of the Yew. It survived the onslaught of the longbow and the destruction of yews, mainly because local people were nervous of the place. It was said that the Tylwyth Teg lived there, and there were fairy circles all over the ground. In the middle of this wood, the greatest yew tree of all was said to spread its great branches over a fairy circle called the Dancing Place.

Many years ago, two farmworkers, Iago and Twm, went out to the Forest of the Yew to do some work on a mild winter's day. Early in the afternoon the mist rose from the ground and the sky became a little too dark for comfort.

'Sun must be setting already,' said Iago.

'Reckon we should make for home,' said Twm.

They retraced their steps, with leaves and twigs crunching under their feet, until they came to a great yew tree in the middle of the woods. This place was still and calm, and the mist had lifted. The air was bright with winter sun, and the water glistened from every dark frond of the yew. The tree's berries gleamed red and bright.

They had been too hasty – it wasn't getting dark at all. They couldn't go home yet! So they both sat down with their backs against the great yew trunk and decided to take a nap.

After some time Twm woke up and looked around. Iago was gone!

'That's not like him,' said Twm. 'I must have been asleep longer than I thought. Perhaps he's gone back to the village already.' So Twm walked home through the twilight and if anyone asked him where Iago was, he said, 'He went home earlier.'

But Iago was still missing the next morning, and now Twm was questioned closely about what had happened. He confessed about the nap under the great yew tree. They searched for Iago through the forest and the whole district, and after a few days Twm went to the local gwr cyfarwydd (conjuror).

The conjuror looked worried. 'There is only one thing you can do. Go to the same place where you and Twm slept. It's the Dancing Place. Go there exactly a year after he was lost, on the same day, and at the same time. Whatever you do, DO NOT step into the fairy ring. The boy will come out to dance. When he gets close to you, snatch him out of there as quickly as you can.'

A long year's wait later, Twm stood within a safe distance of the great yew, on the same day, at the same time as the year before. This time, a light rain pattered on the dark green fronds of the yew.

Merry music started from somewhere below the ground and Iago appeared, dancing madly under the tree with all the little people of the Tylwyth Teg. They were no taller than his knee, whirling shadows of brown and gold and green. Twm took a deep breath and, without stepping forward, he reached out for Iago's hand to pull him clear.

The two lads both flew back and landed hard on the forest floor, and instantly the music stopped. Twm looked at Iago. He was a thin, pale heap of a skeleton, with little energy to collect himself. 'What have they done to you?' cried Twm. 'Did they not give you food?'

'No,' said Iago, staggering to his feet, 'but I'm sure I had some food in my pockets.' He pulled out both his pockets but they were empty. 'Strange, I was sure I'd got food this morning before I came out. Oh, well, time for home.'

Iago had no idea that he'd been away dancing for a full year. As soon as he returned home and tasted food, his poor body withered away to nothing.

THE APPLE TREE MAN

Apples and apple trees appear in many stories about care of the land and of nature, and often they provide protection as well. This story, collected in Somerset by folklorist Ruth Tongue around 1920, is one of my favourites: wassailing, magic, herbs and apples in one tale!

'Borough English' was a local inheritance custom in the countryside, where the main inheritance came to the youngest son; the

older siblings were already meant to have made their way in the world. 'Fingers-and-thumbs' is a local Somerset name for bird's foot trefoil, which is also called 'bird's eye' and 'eggs-and-bacon'.

There was an old farmer who had two sons. The elder was hard working and thoughtful in his words and deeds. He had a love of the land, of nature and the old ways, which made his life rich; his pockets never jangled with coins, but he never really minded about that. The younger son was very different: he was spoiled and greedy. He expected everything to be done the way he wanted, and he had little honour about him. And the two brothers had no love for one another.

The old man died one year in high spring, and it was the custom in that part of the country that the youngest son got all the inheritance: the big house, everything in it, all the land, and all the animals. He made great play of giving bits and pieces to all his wider family, but he also delighted in his new power to make his elder brother feel small and worthless. His brother got the castoffs and worn-out things: his dad's old moth-eared donkey, an ox that had all gone to skeleton and sores, and a tumble-down old shack and outhouse with a scant bit of grass and two or three groaning old ancient apple trees nearby, all that remained of an orchard where his dad had once lived with his grandfather. But the cottage was only rented to the elder brother. The younger one made sure that he always got the rent in full, and that the elder brother took it up to the big house on time every month.

It wasn't the best situation, but the elder brother didn't grumble. He rolled up his sleeves and set to work. He went out along the lanes to cut lush grass for the two animals, and cut ash, elm, holly and ivy for leaf fodder. He gathered the gentler healing herbs from the springtime hedgerow – clover, goose-grass, fingers-and-thumbs – and he made sure there were plenty for the animals to eat. The ox and the donkey began to fatten up and brighten up nicely. With advice from the local wise woman he sought out burdock, comfrey and nettle, and mashed them up into a poultice to put on the poor old ox's sores, saying the right words as he did so. That old ox picked himself up and walked smart and strong.

Then he turned the beasts into the orchard, and all the goodness and herb magic came out of the other end of the animals, and it treated the land, and the gnarly old apple trees flourished a marvel. The trees were struggling under the weight of the mistletoe, so he cut a lot of the good mistletoe to sell at the market the following winter. He then carefully pruned the apple trees, which would strengthen them in time, but he knew it would take years before they fruited well again.

None of this helped the elder brother get his rent together and look after himself, and life became more and more difficult. He did some work up at the farm next door, but it didn't bring in much. By the end of the second year, he had used any savings he had, and he was barely scraping together enough money to pay for rent and food.

Then one day the younger brother came along, the first time he had ever visited his sibling's home since their father died. He said, 'It'll be Christmas Eve soon, when they say the beasts can talk at midnight. I've heard them tell down in the village that there's treasure around here somewhere, and so I'm set to ask your donkey when he can talk – I reckon he's got more brains than the other one. He'll know that he has to tell me the truth, if he knows what's good for him, because I'm the owner of this place.' The donkey and the ox both stopped munching on their hay and eyed him suspiciously, but he didn't notice.

The younger brother poked the elder in the ribs a little more than playfully. 'It'll be your lucky Christmas – 'cause if you come up to the big house and wake me just before midnight on Christmas Eve, so that I can come and listen to the animals, I'll take sixpence off your rent for January. But if you don't wake me, then I might just find myself a new tenant. Got that?' And he walked off, whistling a little tune.

Christmas was a soggy affair that year, and by the time the sun had gone as low in the sky as it would and the celebrations were due, the constant rain had soaked all the cheer out of the elder brother. On Christmas Eve, he determined to do something about it. That evening, he went out to the shed and gave the donkey and the ox a little bit of extra food, and then he opened the cupboard in his kitchen and got out the last bit of the year's cider. He mulled the cider over the little kitchen ash-wood fire, using bits of cinnamon and clove, and then he poured it into his mug and took it outside to the orchard.

It was still slating with rain, and perishing cold, and the water soon ran in rivers down the elder brother's neck and into his raggedy shirt. But no matter. He went up to the biggest and the oldest of the ancient apple trees, pulled an old hard crust of bread from his pocket, dunked it in the cider, and put the soaked bread in the crook of one of the tree's branches. Then he started to sing:

> Old apple tree, I wassail thee,
> And hoping thou will bear
> For the lady knows where we shall be
> Till apples come next year.

He tipped the last of the cider at the roots of the tree and continued:

For to bear well and to bloom well
So merry let us be,
Let every man take off his hat
And shout to the old apple tree.
Hats full, caps full, three bushel bags full,
And a gurt heap under the stairs.
Hurray!

This last cheer came from the elder brother's mouth sounding so small in the cold rain, that he didn't have the heart to cheer any more. The rain carried on, and he found himself looking at the apple tree, all its cracked bark and awkward branches and globs of mistletoe, and wondering just how long it had been growing there, what it must have seen.

Then a voice came – a dry, cracked voice. 'Ah, that were a drop o'good.'

The elder brother looked around. He was sure there was nobody else in the orchard. He looked back at the apple tree, and watched as the fissures in the trunk of the old apple tree gnarled themselves into a huge barky grin, with two knots in the wood for beady, pippy eyes.

'Come on, now, yew take a look under this diddicky root of ours, there be treasure right over there,' said the Apple Tree Man, and he waved his branches over to the middle of the orchard.

The eldest brother wasted no time in finding a spade, and dug in the spot. It wasn't long before spade hit metal, and up came a box full of shining gold coins.

''Tis yours and no one else's,' said the Apple Tree Man. 'Put'n away safe, and bide quiet 'bout 'un.'

The elder brother hauled the metal box into an old sack and took it back to his little shack, where he hid it in the kitchen cupboard. Then he returned to the apple tree and said his thanks. ''Tis a pleasure,' said the Apple Tree Man. 'Now go and call your dear brother. 'Tis nearly midnight.'

So the elder brother went to wake his brother up at the big house, and when that was done he went back to his kitchen, took the sack of gold and his few belongings, and started up the road to seek a new life.

Meanwhile, the bleary-eyed younger brother hurried through the pouring rain up to the orchard and into the old cattle shed, just as the church clock struck midnight. He stood close to the faces of the donkey and the ox and looked at them expectantly, with his teeth clattering in his head from the cold.

Sure enough, after some time had gone by, the donkey turned to the ox and said: 'Yew'd know this gurt greedy fool that's a listening to we so unmannerly. He'd want us to tell where treasure is.'

'And that's where he won't never get it,' said the ox. ''Cause someone a took't it already.'

The Travelling Tree

Long ago, before there were waterproof jackets, or weather forecasts, or cars, or electric light, people still needed to travel at night, in all seasons, and often on foot. You didn't do it unless you needed to, but sometimes there was no choice. You were at the mercy of the dark, and the elements, and the wild beasts ... and the plants. Can a tree also be one of the fairies? Well, you tell me. This story comes from Kent.

A man had to travel between two villages one winter's night. It wasn't a very pleasant night; the wind was getting up, the clouds were heavy, and there was a storm in the air; but the man had to get to the next village.

The clouds kept covering the moon, so he couldn't see the road to walk it. Worse than that, he was sure that he wasn't alone. He kept looking over his shoulder, but he couldn't see whether anything was there or not; and he quickened his pace as the wind whipped up. Was that a laugh? Or was it just the wind?

'Everything sounds louder in the dark. It's just an old tree creaking. Don't be so silly,' he told himself. He pressed on. The wind was howling now, and then the rain started, the kind of rain that pelts against your face and makes it sting. He couldn't see anything at all now, and so he tried to find some shelter until the storm blew over.

There weren't any hedgerows around on this land, but he thought he saw a big old tree with its branches flailing in the gale. He struggled towards it, but then the clouds covered the moon, and as far as he stumbled, the tree wasn't there. When he could see again, the tree was further on, and again he stumbled towards it.

This must have gone on for well over a mile, with the tree always seeming just out of his reach, but he pressed on.

Again he heard a low creaking chuckle in the wind. Again he followed, his arms outstretched to reach the tree, but again it was just out of his reach, and he walked on. The rain was trickling down the back of his neck, and starting to soak through his clothes, icy cold; his cheeks were chapped with the wind, and his fingers and toes hurting with cold.

He must have walked at least four miles; but eventually his fingers did touch rough bark and he put his hands on the tree. He sank down against the trunk out of the wind, worn out, and huddled into his sodden cloak to try to get warm.

Then there was a voice: the same low, creaky voice that had laughed. 'I don't know what you plan to do,' said the tree, 'but I'm getting soaked through. I reckon I'm going home to a good warm fire.'

And off it went.

MOSSYCOAT

There are over a thousand species of moss in Britain and Ireland. They are tiny ancient plants, simple in their structure, dependent on water and often ignored. Druids believed that mosses had the power to prevent accidents and misfortunes. At Widecombe-in-the-Moor in Devon, a monument records the efforts of the villagers in collecting sphagnum moss for wound dressings during the First World War.

Versions of the Cinderella story can be found all over the world. This one from Lancashire was collected from a gypsy teller, Taimi Boswell, in 1915 by T.W. Thompson. I like the way that Mossycoat's gift from her mother is alive and green, painstakingly and lovingly made from ancient plants and gossamer thread. From small insignificant things, great achievements can follow. The coat of simple moss creates a magical path for the girl to walk into her future, being nothing more, and nothing less, than herself.

There was a poor old widow-woman who lived in a little cottage. She had a daughter, in the first bloom of youth, and the girl was very beautiful, although she didn't know it. Ever since the girl's birth, her mother had been busy every day collecting plants in the woods, and busy every evening making a special coat for her, and her daughter didn't know about that either.

In the village there was a cunning man. Now some cunning men are good of heart and skilled with herbs and people, but he wasn't one of those. This man fancied himself a great magician, and gave himself airs and graces. He strutted around the place in coloured velvets that had seen better days, with his greasy hair slicked back from his face and his beard all matted and full of bits of food. Everyone knew about him, and most tried to avoid him.

The cunning man went round the village houses every so often, selling charms and spells, and he threw dark words and malcontent at people if they weren't polite to him. And one day he knocked on the door of the old widow-woman's cottage, and the girl opened it.

'Hello, gorgeous,' said the cunning man, 'aren't you a pretty picture now you're all grown up?'

The girl blushed and looked down.

'It's your lucky day,' he said. 'I'm looking for a wife, and now I've found her. You could marry the best man for miles, my dear, a magician no less! And here, he's standing right in front of you! How about it?' He licked his lips in anticipation.

The girl ran upstairs to her mother. 'Mother! That horrid cunning man is at the door, and he says he wants to marry me!'

'Well, do you want to marry him?' asked her mother.

'No.'

'Tell him that you won't marry him unless you have the right dress. One made of white satin, all embroidered with sprigs of gold. And it's got to fit you just right.'

'But, Mum …'

'Do as you're told now, and trust me.'

So the girl told him what her mother had said. The cunning man chuckled, and hummed, and drooled slightly as he looked the girl up and down to get an idea of her measurements. 'I'll be back right soon enough, and then we can marry.' And he strolled off down the path whistling a little tune.

A week later he was back, with a parcel for the girl. 'Now, how about it?' he said, his dark eyes twinkling. She ran upstairs to her mother with the parcel.

'Try it on,' said her mother.

The dress fitted perfectly. The girl looked in the mirror and could hardly believe the beautiful creature reflected back at her. But there was fear in the girl's eyes.

'Mum, he's waiting downstairs, what should I do?'

'Tell him you need another dress for going away in. This time it should be made of silk, of the colour of all the birds of the air, and it has to fit you just right.'

The girl went downstairs and told the cunning man, and he agreed. A week later he was back with another parcel, and the girl ran upstairs to her mother while he waited at the door. The dress fitted exactly, and it made the girl look even more lovely.

'What should I do now?' wailed the girl. 'I don't want to marry him!'

'Trust me,' said her mother. 'Tell him you need a pair of silver dancing shoes, and they must fit you just right.'

The girl told the cunning man about the shoes. The cunning man spat into the garden, looked at her feet and measured them up in his mind's eye, and said, 'I will be back with them in a week, and then, my dear, we shall be wed, it is agreed.'

She watched him aghast as he walked down the kitchen path.

In a few days, there he was with the shoes. They glittered and sparkled silver in the light, and they fitted her exactly; they were not too tight, nor were they too loose.

Again the girl asked her mother what to do.

'I'm making a special coat for you, that I'll finish tonight, and after that you won't need to worry about him,' said her mother. 'Tell him you will marry him tomorrow, and he should be here at ten o'clock. And mind you don't oversleep tomorrow morning.'

So the girl told him to be back at ten o'clock. 'I'll be here, my love, I can't wait,' said the cunning man, and his face crinkled into a wicked grin, and his eyes blazed.

That night the mother worked right through the dark hours, cutting and sewing and cutting and sewing, until at last the girl's coat was finished, and she went outside and held it up to the dawn light as the sun rose. The coat was made of green feathery moss from the woods, and gold thread as fine as gossamer, and nothing else. It shimmered with all the shades of green as living sprigs of moss

peeped through the golden threads. The mossy fabric was as light as down, and as comforting as earth, and as flowing as water.

'This is Mossycoat,' she said early the next morning to her daughter, whose eyes were round with wonder. 'That shall also be your name from now on: Mossycoat.' It was a magic coat, a wishing coat, she explained, and when Mossycoat was wearing it, she only had to wish to be somewhere and she would be there that very instant.

'Now,' said her mother. 'We don't have much time. Today is the day you must go into the world and seek your fortune. And I can see that it will be a handsome fortune indeed.' And Mossycoat knew then that her mother was a cunning woman, who was sound of heart and skilled with herbs and people.

Mossycoat put on her coat under her working clothes, where it was thin as silk and light as a feather. She packed her two dresses and the silver dancing shoes in a big bag, and now she was ready.

'How about the horrible man?' asked Mossycoat.

'Oh don't worry, I'll deal with him. Now, you must wish yourself a hundred miles away, and walk along the road you find until you come to a great hall. You must knock at the door and ask for a job. They will find you work.'

For the last time Mossycoat did as her mother told her, and soon she found herself in front of a big gentleman's house with grand gardens. She opened the gate, walked up the path and knocked at the door, and she told the maid that she was looking for work. The mistress of the house herself came out to see Mossycoat; and she liked the look of her.

'What work can you do?' she asked.

'I can cook, your ladyship,' said Mossycoat, 'in fact I'm a very good cook, from what people have said.'

'I can't give you a job as a cook,' said the mistress, 'as I've got one already; but I could employ you as assistant to the cook.'

'Thank you ma'am, I'd like that,' said Mossycoat.

So it was settled that Mossycoat was to be under-cook. After the lady had showed her to her bedroom, she took her to the kitchen and introduced her to the other servants.

'This is Mossycoat,' she said, 'and I've employed her to be under-cook.'

Mossycoat went back up to her room to unpack and to hide her dresses and silver slippers, and her mossy coat, under the bed.

It goes without saying that the other kitchen girls were wild with jealousy; and it didn't help matters that Mossycoat was a sight more lovely than any of them. How had this new girl, come in fresh from the road in working rags, been set above them, when they (who really knew about everything) had not been asked?

But they would put her in her place.

When Mossycoat came downstairs ready to start work, they set on her. 'No fear of you being under-cook, my dear. We've seen your sort before, full of airs and graces. All you're fit for is to scour pans, clean knives, and clear the drains; and all you will get in return is this.' And the cook came down hard on Mossycoat's head with the greasy skimmer for the top of the fat, *crack*! 'That's what you deserve, and that's what you will get. My *lady*.'

That's how it was for Mossycoat. She was put to do all the dirtiest work, and soon she was up to her ears in grease, and her face was filthy. Every now and again, first one and then another of the servants would fetch her a whack across the head with the skimmer, until poor Mossycoat's head was so sore she could hardly bear it. But the bruises were hidden by her hair, and Mossycoat tried to be as small and as incon-spicuous as she could.

Time went on, and the master and mistress of the house announced there was to be a big dance, that was to last for three nights, with hunting and other sports in the daytime. All the important people for miles around were to be there; and the master, and mistress, and the young master – they only had one child – were very excited about it.

The dance was all the talk among the servants. If only they had the clothes, they said, they would be all right, for they considered themselves as good as high-titled ladies any day. 'And you, Mossycoat, you'd like to go, wouldn't you now?' they cried, and down came the skimmer hard on her head, *crack*! And all of them laughed, except for Mossycoat.

But no amount of dirt could hide Mossycoat's beautiful face, and her quiet and sweet nature. The master and mistress of the house noticed her, and as the dance approached they sent for her and said, 'Mossycoat, would you like to come to the dance?' 'No thank you,' said Mossycoat, 'I know my place better than that. Besides, anyone I got close to would get all greasy and dirty. It's very kind of you, but I won't go to the dance.'

When she got back to the kitchen, they were all over her with questions. Had she been given notice? 'The master and mistress asked me if I'd like to go to the dance,' said Mossycoat. 'What? You?' cried the other servants. 'That's unbelievable. If it had been one of us, then that would be understandable; but YOU? They would need to hold their noses if they so much as got anywhere near you. You must be lying.' Then down came the skimmer on Mossycoat's head, *crack*!

Well, the first night of the dance was such a success; the next night the master and mistress of the house, and their son as well, all asked Mossycoat again if she wanted to go to the dance that evening. Again she refused. 'Listen to her!' cried the other servants. 'Who does she think she is? It's all lies.' There were more bruises to poor Mossycoat's head.

But Mossycoat had already decided that she would go to the dance that night, in proper style, all on her own, and without anybody knowing. She crept upstairs and put on her magical coat of moss under her usual clothes, and then she went down to the kitchen and cast a spell. All the servants were put into a trance as soon as she touched them, unable to wake up again on their own. Then she went back upstairs again, and she had a bath and a really good wash.

Mossycoat then put on her white silk dress with the gold sprigs, and her silver slippers, of course with the mossy coat on underneath. As soon as she was ready, she wished herself at the dance, and found herself tripping up the steps to the ballroom in her silver dancing shoes, with everyone gaping at this beautiful young stranger.

Once young master caught sight of her he couldn't take his eyes off her; he'd never seen a girl so gorgeous before, nor so beautifully dressed. 'Who is she?' he asked everyone he could find, but nobody knew.

'Can't you find out, Mother – can't you go and talk to

her?' His mother went to introduce herself to the young lady and asked her all about herself, but all the girl would say was that she came from a place where they hit her on the head with a skimmer. In time, the young master himself got the courage to go and introduce himself; but she wouldn't tell him her name, and she refused to dance.

He kept coming back, and kept asking. At the end of the evening, she finally agreed, and they danced one turn up and down the room. Then she said she had to go, and rushed outside; he ran after her, but she had vanished into thin air. Nobody had seen where she went, and nobody could find her anywhere, search as they might.

Mossycoat had wished herself back in her room, and her coat made sure it was done. She changed into her working clothes, hid her finery under the bed, then she went back down to the kitchen where the servants was still frozen to the spot. She touched each of them in turn, and they woke up, wondering what time of day it was, and how long they had been asleep.

Well, she told them, and she dropped a hint that she might have to let the mistress know; they begged her not to tell, and offered her things – an old skirt, stockings, stays. So Mossycoat promised she wouldn't tell on them, and they didn't hit her over the head with the skimmer that night.

All next day, the young master couldn't settle his mind for thinking about the mystery girl. He'd fallen in love with her at first sight. He was wondering all the time whether she would be at the dance on the third night, and whether she would vanish afterwards just the same, and how he could stop her. And he couldn't stop talking about her.

Well, the talk reached the ears of the servants. 'To think, Mossycoat, he wanted *you* to go to the dance last night!' they said. 'You've missed your chance!' And they laughed, and they told her she had lied, and they hit her over the head with the skimmer and tipped the contents of the pigswill bin all over her. It was the same again later on, when the master and mistress called Mossycoat and asked her if she would like to go to the dance, and once again she refused. 'It's your last chance, Mossycoat!'

Later that evening, when all the servants had been put under a trance-spell, Mossycoat cleaned herself up and got changed, this time into the silk dress made of all the colours of the birds of the air, and her silver slippers. She wished with the coat to be at the dance, and she was there. As soon as the young master saw her, he asked his father to send for the fastest horse in his stable, and to keep it standing ready saddled at the front door. Then he went over to talk to her; but he didn't learn any more about the mystery girl than he had done the night before.

He asked her to dance, and at first she refused, but then at the last dance she agreed, saying that she must go just as soon as they had danced the length of the room and back.

This time, he kept hold of her as they went outside. Mossycoat wished herself at home, and at once rose into the air and started to disappear. He tried to keep hold of her, but only caught her slipper as she rose up, and the slipper fell to the floor. He picked it up; but as for catching her, it would be easier to catch up with the wind in a howling gale, than it was to catch the mystery girl.

As soon as she got home, Mossycoat changed into her old things; then she freed the servants from their spell. One offered her a shilling, another half a crown, if she wouldn't tell on them for falling asleep at work; and she promised she wouldn't.

The young master took to his bed the next day, sick for the love of the lady who had lost one of her slippers the night before. The doctor couldn't do anything. So, a message was sent out to try to find the lady who could wear the slipper, as only she could save his life; and if she would come to the big house and if the slipper fitted, he would marry her.

The silver slipper was tiny. Ladies came from near and far, some with big feet and some with small, but none of them with feet small enough to get into the slipper, no matter how much they squeezed and pinched. There were queues of young ladies at the door of the great hall, rich and poor, all eager to try on the slipper.

Of course, all the servants tried, but none of them succeeded. They were asked: was there nobody else, nobody at all, rich or poor? 'No,' they said, 'everyone's tried, except Mossycoat.'

'Mossycoat! Of course. Tell her to come here at once,' said the mistress.

Mossycoat crept into the great hall and sat down in front of them all. She slipped her foot into the slipper easily enough, and it fitted her exactly. The young master jumped out of bed, and was going to take her in his arms.

'Stop!' said Mossycoat. 'Wait a minute.' And she ran from the room.

In a few minutes she came back in her silk dress the colour of all the birds of the air, and wearing her silver dancing shoes. Mossycoat was shining and Mossycoat was beautiful. And, they say, the young master nearly ate her on the spot. But he recovered himself, went down on one knee, and asked Mossycoat to marry him. And she agreed.

After all the excitement and the talk of wedding arrangements had died down, there were one or two things that the master and mistress wanted to know. How did she get to the dance, and back again, so quickly? 'Just wishing,' said Mossycoat; and she told them all about the magic coat of moss that her mother had woven for her. 'That explains everything,' they said.

Then the second question. Where was the place where she was hit over the head with a skimmer? 'Why, that was here, in the kitchens,' she said. They were angry when they heard that, and all the kitchen staff were sacked immediately, and the dogs sent after them to drive them away from the place.

As soon as they could, Mossycoat and the young master of the house got married. They lived happily ever after, and had a basketful of children.

2

THE QUICKENING

As the light grows longer
The cold gets stronger
Let Bride come in
Bride is welcome ...

Hebrides

By the beginning of February, there are signs of life in the plant kingdom. Snowdrops are in bloom, aconites and winter jasmine are on the move, and many trees are thinking about flowering. But the days are still short and it seems to get ever colder. Even though this time is the old celebration of Imbolc, the first of the three spring festivals, springtime has a fragile beginning.

BRIDE AND THE CAILLEACH

The two main characters in this story have many traditions. The Cailleach or Beira, the Celtic hag goddess, represents the harsh state of winter, to be replaced by Bride (sometimes called Bridget or Brig) as springtime emerges. In some stories, the two are the same figure, transforming from maiden to mother to hag as the year progresses.

Snowdrops, also called February fairmaids or Candlemas bells, are in bloom now and they bring the first delicate energy and hope of spring.

The Cailleach was the first of all the gods and goddesses in Scotland, older than even she knew, casting her huge shadow over the land. Her frost-white hair tumbled down her back over a dun-coloured shawl, which was always drawn tight around her shoulders. Her teeth were red and rusty and very sharp.

The Cailleach's one eye surveyed the mountains with sight as keen as ice and as swift as the mackerel in the ocean. She had created this place many years ago, directing her hags to haul creels of rock so that mountains could be piled up to the clouds, and then chipping at the rocks with her magic hammer until she was happy with their form.

And why make the mountains? The Cailleach used them as stepping stones across the land, and also as houses for her giant sons. Each giant was called a Fooar, and they quarrelled constantly, hurling boulders around the land that can still be seen today. The youngest of the Cailleach's sons, Angus Og ('Forever Young'), lived out to the west on the Green Isle, the Land of Youth.

The Cailleach would wander the mountains on stormy nights, singing mournful songs that echoed around the glens. Wherever she hit the ground with her magic hammer, the soil would become hard as iron. When she lost her temper, which was often, she was the fierceness behind the biting north wind, and the anger of the pounding waves.

One day, the Cailleach spied a young girl walking across a glen, and she enjoyed sending the harsh winds to make the girl's journey difficult. But the girl didn't give in, she kept plodding on, with fire in her eyes. 'Ah!' thought the Cailleach, 'another worker for me!' And she swept up the terrified young girl in a gale and lifted her up to her mountain castle, where she was imprisoned and put to work.

The girl's name was Bride, and no matter how hard she worked the Cailleach found fault and made her life a misery. Every day that passed Bride seemed to become stronger and more radiant, and the Cailleach was becoming weaker and weaker. Even worse, Angus Og had dreamed of Bride and he'd fallen in love with her. He kept asking his mother where he could find the beautiful girl from his dream, but the Cailleach had no intention of telling him. The winter storms became more violent, the frost harsher, the waves higher.

One day the Cailleach gave Bride a brown fleece and said, 'You must wash this in the mountain stream until it is pure white.'

Bride took the fleece and went to the stream, and began to wash it in a pool below a waterfall. All day long she washed, her arms aching, her hands turning blue with the cold, but the fleece wouldn't turn a shade lighter. The Cailleach sent Bride out there a second day, and then a third day, washing and scrubbing the brown fleece.

On the third morning, a grey-bearded old man appeared by the pool, and asked Bride: 'Why are you crying?'

Bride explained the impossible task. 'Who are you?' she asked.

'My name is Father Winter,' said the old man, 'here, give me the fleece, I can help.'

He shook the fleece three times, and it became white as new snow. 'Take this back to the Cailleach, and tell her the new herbs and new grass are on the rise.' Bride thanked the old man and walked back to the Cailleach's castle.

When Bride relayed the old man's message to the Cailleach, she howled with anger and called for her eight hags. 'Ride in all the four directions, ride like the wind!' she cried. 'Strike the world with frost and chill, so that no flowers bloom and no blade of grass survives.' Howling winds whipped across the land and blizzards soon followed.

Angus Og sat among the mountains of the Green Isle and watched the storms over Scotland that made travel impossible, even for a giant. He couldn't forget his dream of Bride and he was determined to find her. 'It is the wolf month, and the tempers of wolves are uncertain,' thought Angus. 'I shall cast a glamour on the sea and a glamour on the land, and borrow one day from August.' He worked his magic, and it wasn't long before the ocean was slumbering and the sun was casting shadows with the mountains. Angus rode on his white horse to Scotland, over the Hebrides and the Minch, and across to the Grampian mountains. But Bride was nowhere to be found.

Angus waited in the woods near his mother's castle, and early the next morning, as the chill returned, he noticed a path of little white snowdrops across the woodland floor. Following it, he finally saw Bride, walking through the trees, every footstep causing snowdrops to bloom where she had trodden. Angus hurried to meet Bride and he took her hand. They shared gentle words and great hopes that day, and made a hiding-place in the woods where even the Cailleach couldn't find them. And there, Bride and Angus Og fell in love and made their promises to one another.

The Cailleach rose late the next day, and with her one eye she saw the changes happening across the land. She had no energy in her limbs now, not even enough breath for shouting. She searched everywhere for Bride and Angus without success, and at dusk she threw her magic hammer under a holly tree (that's why nothing grows under the holly). Then

she transformed herself into a barn owl (*Cailleach oidhche-gheal*) and flew silently, weary and ailing, to the Green Isle, the Land of Youth. There, the barn owl swooped down into a glade with a bubbling spring coming from the rocks. This was the Well of Youth, her last hope.

The Cailleach sat silently by the spring all night, watching in her giant form. When the first hint of light rose in the eastern sky, she held the water to her lips and she drank. Then the form of the Cailleach wavered and dissolved in the dawn air, and as it did, a pale green light shimmered across the glade and violets and primroses began to bloom. Catkins appeared on the hazel and fluffy buds on the willow, and the grass and moss pushed up towards the springtime light. Birdsong rang out from among the trees. The rock glistened and sparkled with quartz and mica in the sunshine. In the woods, the new king and queen of springtime, Angus Og and Bride, were filled with new strength and fire and they danced, laughing with the joy of it all.

CROOKER

Plants are not always a protection against evil spirits. Sometimes they can harbour their own malevolent intent, and terrorise a place. This story comes from the Derwent valley in Derbyshire. In 2002, Cromford Parish Council received complaints about the lack of lighting and overhanging shrubbery on the Lea Road, which runs alongside the river Derwent (Darrent) between the station and the old bridge.

A traveller was on his way to Cromford late on a dank winter's day, hurrying to see his sick mother. By sunset he was nearly at the village, when a shadowy old woman approached him on the road. 'Where are you going, so late at night?' she asked. 'We've lost the sun now, and it will soon be dark. You must know that this is no safe road to be travelling on at night.'

She was a curious old woman, dressed in green in some old-fashioned style. The traveller was taken aback, and couldn't think of anything to say. She said, 'I see you are a wise traveller, wise enough not to invite trouble from a stranger. But I doubt very much if you'll be safe from Crooker, without the right kind of help. Here.'

She held out a posy of flowers to him, with straight stems and little starry yellow flowers: it was St John's Wort, completely out of season. He accepted the posy with thanks, and the old woman nodded in satisfaction. 'I wish you well on your journey,' she said. 'A while ago you freed a bird from a fowler's net. I know that bird. Take the flowers, and when you walk along the Cromford Road, show them to Crooker.'

'Who is Crooker?' asked the traveller.

But the old woman had disappeared into thin air. He was all alone with the yellow flowers in his hand.

'That was very strange,' he muttered. 'But I must get to Cromford tonight.' And he carried on walking.

Up ahead a few hundred yards, another old woman was waiting for him on the land side of the road. In the fading light, he could see that she too was dressed in green, and holding a posy of primroses. It was much too early for primroses.

'You should be warned that nobody dares to travel the Cromford Road at night,' she said, 'and there is little light left now.'

'Thank you, but I must press on,' he said, 'my old mother is ill and needs me.'

'I see that you are determined. Then show these primroses to Crooker,' she said, and offered him the posy. 'Some years ago, you freed a hare from a snare. I know that hare. And I'm happy to offer you the right kind of help.'

'Who is Crooker?' asked the traveller.

But she was gone, and he was all alone on the road. 'Hello? Who is Crooker?' he shouted, but there was no response. The traveller quickened his footsteps into the dark.

A little further on, at the corner of the lane, he met a third old woman dressed in green. 'You would do well not to travel the Cromford Road at such a dark and dangerous time as this,' she said.

'So I understand. But I have no choice. I must get to Cromford as quickly as I can,' said the traveller. 'I have an idea you might be able to help me.'

'Yes. You can do with the right kind of help. Take these and show them to Crooker.' The old woman handed the traveller a little posy of daisies, with their petals all folded up for the night.

'Thank you. Who is Crooker?' asked the traveller, but she did not answer. Instead, she said, 'Last year, you freed a vixen and her fox-cub from a trap. I know that vixen and that fox-cub. So, I will give you more advice. Keep as far away from the Darrent river as you can. It's important that you get to the Cromford Bridge and the chapel shrine, before the moon rises and the moonlight shines on the road.'

And then she too disappeared, and there was the traveller all alone with his three posies of flowers. 'Looks like I might need these, then,' muttered the traveller to himself. 'Let's see what's up ahead. But I reckon there's a way to go yet. I doubt I'll reach the bridge before the moon comes up. And the moonlight will come in handy – they say the Darrent runs fast and deep and I don't want to miss my footing.'

When, at last, his weary legs brought the traveller to Cromford Road, the moon was high overhead and casting its white light over the land and the swirling waters of the river Derwent. It was impossible to keep away from the river, as the road ran right alongside it, and there were great black shapes of trees on the bank on the other side. The trees cast looming, muddling shadows that moved across the road in the wind and the moonlight, and their limbs creaked and groaned in the quickening wind. For all it was a bright moonlit night, the air was becoming stormy overhead.

'I don't like it here. I don't like the look of those moving branches,' muttered the traveller. 'Look at that one big tree up ahead, there, it looks for all the world like spindly black hands, clutching at the road. Still, I'm nearly there. I reckon I'll make a dash for it.' And for all his travel weariness, he picked up his pace and ran, until he passed the tree on the road and crossed its shadows.

Then the water of the river began to ripple and slurp, as if it were crying 'HUNGRY! HUNGRY!' and the crooked tree shadows on the road from behind him began to overtake his own shadow on the road ahead, grasping and clawing. The tree nearly had him. 'Crooker,' gasped the traveller, no breath in his lungs, but he kept running. Without looking back he hurled the posy of daisies over his left shoulder onto the road. The shadows disappeared. The Darrent river shouted 'GIVE!' and there was a loud splash.

The traveller kept running, but again the dark shadows of Crooker loomed onto the road ahead of his own, and he hurled the posy of primroses over his left shoulder. Crooker stopped; the Darrent river shouted 'GIVE!' and there was a second splash.

And now the traveller was almost spent, but he was so nearly at the bridge. Here was clawing Crooker on the road behind him, black and grasping at his back, swallowing up his shadow. With the last drop of his energy, the traveller turned

right round and flung the posy of St John's Wort straight at
the wicked tree. It cried out with the creaks and groans of
a thousand branches, and the traveller leapt onto Cromford
Bridge and fell in a faint at the door of the little chapel.

The Darrent river roared and gurgled through the night,
and the good people of Cromford looked at each other pale
with terror. 'Darrent and Crooker are out tonight,' they said.
'Do you remember the old beggar woman we found with
a broken neck in the river, the last time he roared? We will
have to get the priest at sunrise, he will have another dead
body and a poor terrified soul to deal with.'

But when they came to Cromford Bridge the next
morning, in the warmth of the early sun, there was a dirty,
footsore traveller kneeling and saying his prayers at the
door of the chapel shrine. Then he got to his feet and fairly

hobbled up to Cromford, where the Darrent river babbled, innocent and sun-dappled, through the village and down past the bank where a great ash tree stood.

THE FAIRY WIDOWER

Ferns are a primitive group of plants with many species throughout the islands, some deciduous and some evergreen. It's difficult to tell in stories whether references to ferns are for ubiquitous bracken, graceful male fern or tenacious polypody. Some people believed that collecting fern seed would make the collector invisible, and there was a widespread belief across Britain that stepping on a fern would cause a traveller to become confused or lose their way. This story comes from Cornwall, where hart's tongue fern and polypody sprout from the ancient hedgebanks all year round.

Not many years ago, a pretty young girl called Jenny Permuen lived in Towednack. Her parents were poor, and she worked in service; but Jenny always acted above her station. She was always very well turned out and wore flowers in her hair. She attracted a lot of attention from the young men of the parish, and a lot of envy from the young women.

The truth was that Jenny was vain. She loved flattery, and she took any comment or criticism straight to heart. If anyone told her how beautiful she was, she shone. If anyone told her not to believe such shallow nonsense, she would purse her lips and rush to find a mirror to reassure herself that she was, indeed, the most beautiful girl in the village.

One day, Jenny's mother sent her to look for work, as she had not been 'in a situation' for a while. She walked down to the lower villages until she came to the crossroads on the Lady Downs, and she discovered that she didn't know which road to take. Confused, she sat down on a granite boulder near the crossroads and pondered; and she plucked and picked at the fronds of fern that were growing all around the boulder. She looked at the fronds, and looked at her hands and how beautiful they were, and then looked at the fronds of fern again, and wondered how she looked sitting there, in case anyone were to go by and notice her. Jenny was lost in a haze of indifference to anyone but herself.

Eventually she stirred, and turned to get up and walk in some direction or other; and it was then that she saw the young man, who had been a little way off, watching her.

'Well, Jenny,' he said, 'what are you after?'

She was startled. 'I … I'm after a place, sir.'

'And what kind of a place do you want, pretty Jenny?' He flashed her a winning smile, just enough to set her off balance. He was very good looking.

'I'm not particular, sir, I can make myself useful.'

'Indeed,' said the man. 'Do you think you could look after a poor widower with a little boy?'

'Oh yes, sir, I'm good with children.'

'Well, then,' he said. 'I wish to hire a young woman like yourself, for a year and a day, to look after my little boy.'

'Where do you live?' asked Jenny, curious, because she had never seen him before.

'Not far away, I will show you,' he said.

'How did you know my name?'

'I've seen you hereabouts. I watched you one day dressing your hair in the lake, and stealing some of my sweet violets to put in your lovely hair. Now, Jenny Permuen, will you take the place, for a year and a day? And if we are pleased with each other, then we can renew the arrangement after that.'

'What are the wages?'

The widower jangled gold pieces in his breeches pocket. 'Oh, money! Well, whatever you like to ask, Jenny.'

Visions moved in front of Jenny's eyes then, of floaty silk dresses, parties and all kinds of finery. Without any more hesitation she said: 'I'll take it. When shall I start?'

'Right now would be good. My little boy is very unhappy.'

'But my mother ... My clothes ...'

'Don't worry, I'll take care of all of that, and you'll have much better clothes soon. But there is an oath you must swear before you begin.'

Jenny looked frightened at this. 'Don't worry,' he said, kindly, 'there is nothing to worry about. All you need to do is to kiss that fern-frond in your hand, and say, 'For a year and a day, I promise to stay.'

'Oh, is that all?' Jenny kissed the fern-frond. 'For a year and a day, I promise to stay.'

The man didn't say another word, but walked forward, taking the road from the crossroads leading east. Jenny followed him, hurrying as fast as she could to keep up, and they kept on walking, and walking, and the road never seemed to end. Her feet were sore and her legs were aching, and at last she started to cry.

He looked back, and hurried to her side. 'Ah – sit down, sit down,' and he led her to a grassy bank, and took more fern fronds from the base of the bank, and put them over first one of her eyes and then the other.

Jenny's tears and weariness left her in an instant, and she could feel herself travelling, although she knew she was still in the same place. It was dark, and they were travelling deep underground. At last they stopped.

'Now, Jenny, you still have some tears there, and human tears are not allowed to enter our house. Let me dry them for you.' He used the same fern fronds to brush her eyes. When she opened her eyes again, before her was a completely different country. Hills and meadows shimmered with flowers she had never seen before; great mountains of granite sparkled in the sun; rivers and waterfalls were set with rainbows; and people everywhere, in clothes of green and gold, were singing and telling stories. It was a merry place.

'It's good to be home,' said the man, and Jenny turned to see that he had changed; he was now wearing a green coat embroidered with gold and gems. 'Now, you must meet my son.' He led Jenny into a great house, with furniture all inlaid with pearls and silver, until they came to a room hung with lace worked with flowers. There in the middle of the room was a cot made out of a huge mother-of-pearl shell, and inside was a little boy so pretty that Jenny cried out with delight.

'Here is your charge,' said the man. 'I am the king of this place, and I want my son to know about human nature. All you have to do is to wash and dress him when he wakes up in the morning, take him outside for walks, and put him to bed when he's tired.'

Jenny did exactly as she was asked, and she enjoyed every single minute. She loved the little boy, and he appeared to love her as well; and the days and weeks and months flashed by quickly.

One morning Jenny woke up and all had changed. She was back in her mother's cottage in Towednack, and everything was strange to her, and nobody knew who she was. She stayed in bed, and everyone thought she was an invalid who was sick in her mind, her stories were so strange.

The wise women of the village came in to see her, and Jenny told them the same tale as she had told everyone else.

'There's a test for this,' said one of the old women. 'Jenny, sit up in bed and crook your arm.'

Jenny crooked her arm and put her hand on her hip.

'Now say, "I hope my arm never comes uncrooked if I have told you a lie".'

'I hope my arm never comes uncrooked if I have told you a lie.'

'Uncrook your arm now, Jenny,' said the old woman.

Jenny unbent her arm.

'She's telling the truth,' said the old woman, 'she's been carried away by the Small People.'

'Is there anything that can cure her mind?' asked one of the others.

'All in good time. I'm sure that her master will make sure she never wants,' said the old woman.

But they say that Jenny lived an unhappy life. She married, and yet she always pined after the fairy widower, and walked with melancholy all her days.

THE BASKETMAKER'S DONKEY

Basket-weaving is one of the most common crafts in the history of any civilisation, and those of Britain and Ireland are no different. Before the advent of plastic, basket-making used to be a thriving industry, using withies – a number of willow and osier (Salix) species both wild and cultivated. Cut willow will readily re-grow if planted. This is an old gypsy story.

In the times when most gypsies used to travel with pack-donkeys, there was an old man whose donkey had been with him for so many years that it had become a good friend. The old man used to make a living by making baskets for his wife to sell from house to house, and sometimes pegs, or a few skewers. He was not a full gypsy, but he knew a little of their ways.

One day the old man was sitting outside at his basket-weaving, and his donkey was keeping him company, as usual. But unlike its normal quiet self, the donkey kept fussing and braying, putting him off his work, and disturbing his concentration. At last the old man grew angry, and picking up a long leather switch, he lashed out at the donkey, hitting it with such force that it cut the poor beast clean in two.

The old man was beside himself with grief and tears, and he did the only thing he knew. He to fetch a new bundle of willow-withies. He stood up the two halves of the donkey, and wove them tightly together with the withies, and filled in all the joins with clay.

To his great joy, over the next few days the two halves joined together and grew again, and the old donkey was revived. In fact, the donkey lived as long as its master. Even better, the willow-withies grew as well, and provided plenty of raw material for the old man's baskets after that.

MAON AND THE WILLOW

Willow is associated with the goddess and the feminine mysteries in many of our traditions, but it often gets a bad press in stories – think of Old Man Willow in Tolkien's Lord of the Rings, *or the Whomping Willow in Rowling's Harry Potter books. I like*

the following story because it is a little more generous. It's a story which has many other versions all over Britain, but this one is from Ireland.

Willow, of course, has ears, and here it also has the gifts of voice and honesty and freedom that run as a thread throughout the tale of Maon. The Brian Boru harp from the Middle Ages, now kept at Trinity College Dublin, has a sound-body made of willow.

Covac stole the throne of Ireland. He killed the king, and the king's son Ailill; and he tortured the king's grandson, Maon, who was the rightful heir to the throne. Maon had always worn a big floppy hat as long as anyone had ever known. Nobody knows the terrors that little Maon had to endure during his torture, or whether they involved his floppy hat, but one result was that he no longer spoke.

Times got a little better for Maon when his supporters smuggled him to Munster, to the kingdom of Fermaroc. There he was allowed to be a child, and played with the daughter of Fermaroc, princess of Munster, whose name was Moriath. A little time after, he was smuggled again to Gaul, his great-grandmother's country, where he lived in exile and grew up to be a noble youth, albeit a silent one. Moriath continued to nurse her love for Maon until she was a young woman, and then she decided to act on her feelings.

Moriath was determined to bring Maon back to Ireland so that she could be with him, and so that he could claim his birthright. She wrote a ballad, a love song, and asked the king of Ulster's bard, Craftiny, to compose the music to match her words. Then she gave the bard rich gifts and sent him to France, where he played the harp and sang the song to Maon.

The song enchanted Maon's heart and stirred his soul, so much that he exclaimed, 'How much love I hear in this music!' And from then on, Maon started to talk again.

Now that Maon was gaining in strength and spirit, his advisors told him the truth about his family and that he was the rightful king of Ireland. The king of France supplied him with an army, and he returned to Ireland in full battle strength. Without even announcing his identity, Maon challenged Covac in his own court, surprised him and killed him single-handed in battle. The people of the court wondered who this fierce warrior with a big floppy hat could be.

The king's druid, ever observant, thought that he might know the answer. 'What is his name?' he asked one of the French warriors quietly.

'We know him only as Maon, the mariner.'

The druid then turned to Maon. 'Have you always spoken with the voice you have now?'

'In truth,' said Maon, 'I have only been speaking again for about a year. Before that, I only remember being silent.'

And from that day the rightful king of Ireland was known as Maon Labraidh, the Mariner Who Speaks. He married his true love, Moriath, the princess of Ulster, and they lived happily ever after – for the next ten years.

But our story doesn't quite end there. There was one thing that Maon never spoke about, one dark secret that he never revealed. For the truth was that Maon Labraidh had embarrassingly long ears. They had grey silky fur like a donkey's, and were altogether unkingly. Maon hid them successfully under his trademark hat. The only person who knew about Maon's ears was his wife and queen, Moriath, and she could be trusted not to tell.

But there was a problem. Every so often, Maon's hair had to be cut, and the man to do this was chosen by lots, for he was put to death afterwards so that Maon's secret would never be known.

One year, the son of a poor widow was chosen for the task, but his mother begged and begged for her son to be allowed to live, pleading that he was the most trustworthy of the king's subjects. King Maon agreed on one condition: that the man would swear by the sun and the wind never to tell a living person what he might see. And so the young man swore the oath, cut the king's hair, and then returned to his mother.

But the secret of King Maon's ears stayed inside the young man, and the secret grew, and the secret became a heavy burden. The weight of it began to tire him out, then wear him down, then eat him up, and eventually he became ill. Finally his mother sought the advice of the king's druid, in secret, because she was fearful of repercussions.

'That's easy,' said the druid. 'He must go to a far away place in the wood, and he must go to the tree that he feels attracted to. Then he should whisper his secret to the tree.'

The sick young man, with the last of his strength, wandered out into the wild woods surrounding the king's court, and there he found a gnarly old willow tree, with fissured bark and spreading branches. He put his lips to the bark of the tree and whispered very quietly, hardly daring to be heard, 'The king has donkey's ears.'

There was silence, and he said it again, very quietly; and the young man felt somehow lighter for the telling of it. By the time he got back to the king's court he was completely recovered.

All went well for three years or so, until one day the king's harpist, Craftiny, the one who had helped the king regain his true voice, and the king and Moriath to find each other all that time ago, decided that he needed a new harp.

Craftiny walked the wildwood for miles, asking the place for advice and searching for the right tree to give its precious wood for the new instrument. And the tree he found was that same old willow.

The new harp was made, and it was truly handsome. The day came for it to be played for the first time. These days were important times in the lives of the bards, and so the king, the queen and all of the court were assembled in the great hall to listen.

Craftiny put his fingers to the fine golden strings and began to play. But there was no harp music, no fine clear notes from strings plucked by skilful fingers. Instead, ringing around the hall, so that the furthest heard it as loudly as the nearest, was a new song. The words of the new song were, 'The king has donkey's ears! The king has donkey's ears!'

The king's harpist stopped playing and the hall fell silent. All eyes were on the king. After a pause, he decided there was only one thing he could do. He stood up from his great chair, took his hat off, and – there were his furry grey donkey's ears standing proud and tall in front of all the assembled court.

A snigger started in the crowd, followed by a chuckle, then a chortle, and soon the whole of the great hall was ringing with the sound of the court's laughter. The king went bright red in the face, but stood still and proudly in front of his people.

Then gradually, the laughing changed, and someone started to clap. To applaud. People all across the room rose to their feet and clapped their hands together in appreciation of their fine king, their mariner king, their king who found his voice, their king who did not run away in shame, and was not afraid to stand up in front of them with his affliction. People started shouting out, 'Hail the king! Hail our excellent king!'

We will leave them, there, celebrating in the great hall of the court of King Maon Labraidh. I am sure that, somewhere in that crowd, there was one very relieved young man.

3

Struggle and Hope

It isn't spring until you can plant your foot
on twelve daisies.

Cambridgeshire

Towards the end of March, it is equal day and night at the
equinox, and we can look forward to longer days. At the
tipping point between winter and springtime there are still
no leaves on the trees, but the herbs in the hedgerows and
the meadows are all pushing their way towards the gentle
sunshine – when the snow and the rain don't get in the way.
Humans are also starting to move, to welcome in the spring,
to begin all the hard work of the year to come.

THE GREEN MIST

Cowslips, along with violets, are the first flowers I remember.
Their delicate scent and modest flowers are a springtime treat.
Folklore, however, tells of sadder times. This story comes from
Lincolnshire.

In the old days, there were bogles, the horrid things, creeping in the darkness, ready to take people. And even in the daytime, when there weren't bogles, people were always fretting about them, or something or other else – or the Church was worrying for them. The priests were always on at people about their souls, and between hell and the bogles, people's minds were never easy.

Still the old traditions carried on, no matter what the Church said. People would still put bread and salt on the flat stones in the lane to get a good harvest; they would smear blood on the door-sill to keep away the horrors; and they would welcome in the Oak King together with the Christ at Yule-time. All the traditions got mixed up, and nobody thought any the worse of it. And one of the most important traditions was welcoming in the springtime.

At the beginning of spring the folk who believed in the old ways went to every field in turn, and lifted a clod of earth from the land; and they said strange and queer words, that they didn't even understand themselves, words that had been said for hundreds of years. And every morning at first dawn, they stood on the doorstep, with salt and bread in their hands, watching and waiting for the green mist to rise from the fields and tell them that the earth was awake again, the life was back in the trees and plants and seeds, that spring was truly beginning.

Well, one family who had done this year after year down the generations, had a lot of trouble one winter. There had been sickness through the family; and the daughter, a maid usually in rude health, had grown thin and white like a bag of bones, and she wasn't getting any better.

Day after day she grew paler, until she didn't even have the strength to stand on her feet, and she could only lie at the window watching the winter creep away.

'Oh, Mother,' she kept saying, 'if I could only wake the spring with you again, perhaps the green mist would make me well and bring me energy, like it does the land and the trees and the plants.'

And the mother would comfort her, and tell her not to be so silly, that she would be there to welcome the spring in, and be back to her old self. But the mother watched her daughter day after day, and dread started to grow in her heart. The girl was fading away like a snowflake in the weak sun; and, day after day, the winter dragged on and the spring was getting closer. And every day, the girl asked to be brought to the window so that if the green mist came, she could toss out the bread and salt on the earth with her own poor thin hands.

And still the days went by, with the people watching, but there was no green mist. One evening, the girl said, 'If it doesn't come at dawn tomorrow, then I can't wait for it any longer. The earth is calling me, and the seeds will bloom over my head in short time, I know it well, Mother. And yet, if I could only see the spring waken one more time, I swear – I'd ask no more than to live as long as one of those cowslips that grow every year by the gate, and to die with the first of them when the summer is in.'

'Shush, shush, girl, don't talk so, for the bogles will hear you!' said the mother, full of fear and dread of what might come the next day.

But the next dawn brought the green mist. It came from the earth and wrapped itself round everything, green as the new grass, and fresh as the young herbs of the springtime. The girl was carried to the window, where she crumbled the bread and salt to the earth with her own hands, and said the old words, and she looked to the land by the gate where the cowslips grew. Then she was carried back to her bed, and she fell into a deep sleep, dreaming of summer and flowers and happiness.

Well, whether it was the green mist or not, the girl from that day grew stronger and prettier than ever, and by the time the cowslips were in bud, she was running round and laughing like a spring sunbeam. But her face stayed pale and drawn, so she seemed like a Will o' the Wyke flitting about. On the cold days she would sit shivering by the fire, with not an ounce of energy about her; but when it was sunny, that made her dance and sing and stretch her arms out to the warmth and the light.

By and by the cowslips came into flower, and the girl started tending them, and sniffing at their gentle scent, and watering them, and talking to them so that her family feared she would become mad. 'I'd pull them up and throw them away if it made you come to your senses!' said her mother. But the girl turned to her and said, 'If you care for me, Mother – never, ever pick one of these flowers; they'll fade soon enough themselves, you know that.' Her mother carried on as normal, and nothing was said to the neighbours.

One day a lad of the village stopped at the gate to chat with the girl, fancying her pretty face, and by and by, while he was gossiping, he picked a cowslip and played with it. The girl didn't see what he had done; but as he said goodbye he gave her the flower, smiling, by way of a present.

She looked at the delicate flower, and up at the lad, and all around at the whirl of green plants and sprouting grass and wild blossoms, and up at the shining yellow sun itself; then all at once she shrank from it all, as if the light she loved was burning into her. She cried out and ran into the house, the cowslip clutched close to her breast.

The girl never spoke again. She lay on the bed, staring at the flower in her hand and fading as it wilted through the day. At dawn the next day, on the bed there lay a shrunken, white, dead thing, with a shrivelled cowslip in its hands. The mother covered her dead daughter's face with a sheet, and she mourned.

The bogles had heard the girl's wish and they had granted it. She had bloomed with the cowslips, and faded with the first of them.

GOBLIN COMBE

Primroses are the first flowers of the true springtime, widely gathered across the islands as Easter gifts. A bunch of fewer than thirteen primroses is considered to be unlucky. Primroses feature in a number of folk tales, sometimes offering protection from fairies, and sometimes causing fairies to be summoned. Cowslips, forget-me-not and stitchwort can all have a similar effect. Goblin Combe is in north Somerset.

It was a sunny spring morning at Easter-time, and a group of children went out to pick primroses. One little three-year-old girl wandered away by herself, distracted by all of the flowers she could gather from the banks and the ground, and she followed her nose right down into Goblin Combe. Being so little, she didn't know any better, and she didn't know of the place's reputation.

When the little one looked up and realised that nothing around her was familiar and she was lost, she burst into tears, and the tears ran down her little face and on to her pinafore. She put her big bunch of primroses down on a rock, as she sat down on the ground with her back against the rock and sobbed and sobbed, scared of being all alone, filling the air with her three-year-old's inconsolable grief.

She didn't know about Goblin Combe, so she didn't know that the rock was an entrance to the fairy realm, and that primroses were a way in. The rock opened up, and there were all the little people rushing out and comforting her. They could see that she was an innocent, and hadn't meant to disturb them; and so they gave her a ball made of pure gold to play with, and danced and sang so that she quite forgot herself, and started to smile, and then to chuckle, and then to laugh, and then to dance with them.

The hours flew by full of curiosity and merriment. In time, though, not even the most determined three-year-old can stay awake, and so the fairies put the bunch of primroses back in her little sleeping fist, and transported her home. Her parents found her sleeping soundly in bed late that afternoon, with the primroses and the golden ball beside her on the pillow.

When the little one woke up and told her parents the story, it was the wonder of the village, and everyone talked about it for weeks. There was a ne'er-do-well in the village, the kind of man who told everyone how much he knew it all, and he fancied getting hold of a golden ball or two. The more everyone else told him what a bad idea it was, and how dangerous Goblin Combe could be, the more he was determined to do it.

So he picked a bunch of primroses, and he went down to Goblin Combe, although his way was blocked at times by fallen branches and holes in the ground and dark foreboding sounds coming from behind the banks. He was glad enough to get to the rock, after all he had seen and heard on the way down; and he still had his primroses, and he set them down on the rock.

Well, it wasn't the right day, and he wasn't the right one, and he didn't pick the right number of primroses. As soon the flowers touched the rock, it opened up, and a black-clad arm reached out, picked him up by the scruff of the neck, and dragged him inside. The rock closed with a crack. He was never seen again.

THE BLACKTHORN TREE

Blackthorn is said to be a keeper of dark secrets, and bad tempered if you're not careful. The term 'blackthorn winter' described the blackthorn tree's habit of coming into blossom just before a harsh cold snap arrived in the spring weather. This story comes from Oxfordshire.

There was a farmer, and those who farmed around him doubted his commitment to the job. 'That one's just in it for the money,' they said. 'That one shouldn't be given care of the land, not if it's to be looked after proper.'

Well, there was a big blackthorn tree right in the middle of one of this farmer's fields. That's quite an unusual thing, to find a blackthorn tree on its own, growing proud from its gnarled, bossed old trunk. Goodness knows how long it had been growing there.

The blackthorn tree blossomed in the early spring, always after an unusually mild spell and just before a return to freezing and blustery weather came along. In the spring it sent out many little green leaves to hide its long, sharp thorns; and in the autumn it produced an abundance of little, round, hard, cloudy black fruits, which the farmer's men would gather when he wasn't looking. The tiny birds made their home there, and the little animals made the most of the fruits. Everyone knew the blackthorn tree.

One spring morning, just after the blossom on the tree had come out, the farmer announced, 'That blackthorn tree is coming down today. Damn thing is nothing but a nuisance.' He called to his farm hands to help him out, but they all refused.

'You bloody fools,' said the farmer. 'What's your problem?'

One of the men looked bashful. 'Well, there's fairies look

after that tree. They bury their gold there. It brings luck to the farm. I'll play no part in harming that tree.'

The other men murmured their agreement.

'Ha!' said the farmer. 'Fairies? Gold? You idiots. This is my land. If there is any gold, it's mine. There are no fairies. What a load of old rubbish.'

So, all on his own, the farmer took an axe to the luck-tree that was, unknown to him, the life of the farm. The axe chopped, and chopped, and the sap of the blackthorn tree ran red like blood and still the farmer chopped. Then the blackthorn fell, but not before a good few long sharp thorns had made bloody work of the farmer's fingers and ripped at his clothes.

Once the tree was down, and lying sorry on the ground, the farmer couldn't help himself: he dug under the roots of the tree to see whether there was any gold. But there wasn't any, only a heap of withered leaves.

'A load of rubbish,' said the farmer. 'Just like the fairies.'

Then he turned around and there was his whole farm burned to nothing but glowing ash, and a laughing voice said, 'What a load of old rubbish.'

BETTY STOGS AND THE FAIRIES

There are stories from all over Britain and Ireland about changelings – babies being taken away, or replaced by fairy children. This one, from Cornwall, is a gentle tale that talks about the land as well as care for the child, and it's pretty straightforward in its judgement. Gin lovers beware.

It's well known in parts of Cornwall that the fairies will take away the children of lazy, dirty mothers, and care for them tenderly before returning them with a sharp lesson. And it was in this way that Betty Stogs nearly lost her baby.

Betty's father was an old farmer called Bal, who farmed a few acres, and worked for another farmer as well. Betty, the only child, stayed at home in the daytime as she was growing up, cutting furze and turf, but in the evening she went to church meetings, and she was sharp and clever in her words.

At these meetings she met a man called Jan the Mounster, who sized her up and decided she would inherit, and that she was worth getting to know. So he pretended to be interested in the meetings, and he and Betty became close. It wasn't too long before she discovered she was with child, and her parents, anxious for an honourable future for their only daughter, made all kinds of promises to Jan, who eventually agreed to marry Betty if her parents would give them the great polished copper warming-pan to hang up opposite the door of the cottage.

In its due time the baby was born, but by now Betty herself, as well as her new husband, were becoming the worse for wear. Jan worked as little as possible on the local farm, and drank hard every evening with his mates. Betty had also taken to drink, under the influence of a friendly pedlar woman who sold crotcheted blankets from door to door, with a bottle of gin underneath them in her basket.

The pedlar woman came to the cottage one morning when Betty was making bread. She stayed for a while, and both she and Betty drank a noggin of gin, forgetting both the dough and the baby. When the baby grew crotchety, Betty gave it Jan's watch to play with. Soon the watch had been thrown down into the ashes of the fire, and although Betty tried to save it by washing it in the dishwater, it was never revived. Jan flew into a temper when he came home from his day's work, and the bread was so hard that Jan couldn't get into it with his wood-axe, let alone eat it.

The next morning, Jan took his watch to St Ives to get it fixed, and the watchmaker declared that it was irreparable. There were more fights; and after that Jan and his wife got worse and worse, regularly getting so drunk that the baby was neglected. Sometimes it was left alone for hours on end, crying or not.

One night Betty and Jan came home late from the local alehouse, and the cot where they had left the baby was empty. They were distraught, despite their drunkenness. They searched all night, through the village and the woods, and all over the shore. There wasn't a trace of the baby, and they were heartbroken, for they loved the little one, in spite of treating it so badly. By morning, they were both sitting with their heads in their hands in their little cottage, in despair next to the empty cradle.

The cat came into the room, mewing loudly, and it would not stop, running round and round the two of them sitting there. At last they got up and followed it to a furze bush outside, where the cat stopped. There, on a patch of green moss in the middle of all the furze, was the baby, carefully wrapped, clean, dry and sleeping contentedly. Inside

the wrappings there were flowers of all sorts – violets, primroses, wallflowers, mint and balm, scented and fresh and
bright.

The old people in the village said that the fairies had taken
the child, and that sunrise had interrupted their help; they
were sure the fairies would return to take the child for good
the next night.

Well, the fairies never came back, but the fright it put into
Betty and Jan changed them for good. They cared for their
child, kept their place clean, stopped drinking every day,
worked harder and lived much more happily as a little family
after that.

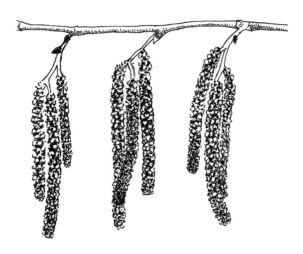

NO MAN'S LAND

In the heavily farmed lowlands of Britain, the one single factor that determines the fate of most of our plants is land ownership. Since at least 1066, this highly political issue of power and money – control over the ultimate fabric of our countryside – has directly influenced the space allowed for wild and cultivated plants to grow, and it has created both misery and wealth in various measure.

With this in mind, it's great to find a story about generosity and sharing the land. The meadow of this heartwarming little tale is now a Site of Special Scientific Interest.

In Tatworth in south Somerset, there is a wet meadow called Stowell's Meadow, or No Man's Land. A stream of the river Axe runs through it, and it has one of the best watercress beds in the district.

Every year this meadow comes up for auction by candle, and here's how it works. A one-inch candle is lit and everyone makes their bids. Only one bid is allowed per person. Nobody is allowed to cough or sneeze for fear of disturbing the candle and being disqualified. The last person to make a bid before the candle goes out gets the meadow for a year.

One year, many centuries ago, there was an old farmer in Tatworth who had fallen on bad times. If he could get the watercress bed, it would just about put him back on his feet. Everyone else wanted him to have it, but rules were rules, and process was process. When the day of the auction came, only two other men turned up to bid against him.

The auctioneer lit the inch of candle. The first man made his bid quickly, which was kindly of him. But to everyone's horror, the candle started to sputter and flicker as if to go out.

The son of the old farmer dug him in the ribs and he blurted out his bid … and then the candle righted itself again and the flame became steady.

The poor old boy was now in deep despair, as he'd made his bid and there was another man who hadn't spoken yet. The candle had burned down to a quarter of an inch, the flame still strong.

What could the second man do? He couldn't try to cough before he spoke; but surely he couldn't help … a … a … sneeze?

The second man looked at the first man, winked, and crinkled up his nose. Out came his red handkerchief. 'You can't sneeze in here while the candle is lit, it's against the rules,' said the auctioneer. So the second man crept over towards the doorway, handkerchief flapping in the air as he held it to his nose.

The candle flickered, but righted itself again.

The second man had another idea. Unseen by the auctioneer, he signalled out of the doorway to his sheepdog waiting outside, and the dog leapt towards him, barking madly and with his tail wagging nineteen to the dozen.

And the candle went out.

The auctioneer solemnly decreed that a poor dumb animal could not make a bid, and the old farmer was duly given the meadow for the year.

Everyone cheered, and then they all went off for their annual watercress feast. The old farmer never suspected, and his dignity remained intact.

4

JOY AND SUNSHINE

The first of May is Pinch-Bum Day,
The second of May is Sting-Nettle Day.

Sussex

It's May Day, Beltane, high spring, and the plant world is full of energy. Jack-in-the-Green is on the march, and everywhere there are flowers and fresh green leaves. This is a time of celebration and the promise of abundance to come.

THE FAIRY SHAWL

Hawthorn, the fire tree, the fairy tree, doesn't often get the chance to grow into a proper tree – these days we find it in the countryside mainly as part of a hedgerow. Known as 'Poor Man's Bread and Cheese', the leaves are edible, although they're tough after the first flush of spring. The great creamy-white masses of May blossom are always a treat. My grandmother refused to allow may blossom into the house before May Day.

This story is from the Isle of Man, where fairies are often called the Good People. They will bring luck to any houses where food and bathing water is left out for them. The Fenoderee is an ugly furry creature something like a Brownie. He is friendly and helpful, despite his scary appearance, and he likes swinging in elderberry trees.

I love the image of the flower shawl in this story – if you had a wildflower shawl, what flowers would it contain?

Murra was a good girl who grew up on a farm, and she worked hard. She had seven brothers younger than herself, and so there was a lot of work to do; but no matter how long the days, she would always remember to leave buttermilk and soda bread out for the little people every night. Why? Because it was the right thing to do.

As Murra's brothers got a little older, she went looking for work. The first farm door she knocked on, the farmer's wife opened.

'Do you have any paid work?' asked Murra.

'Can you spin?' asked the farmer's wife.

'Yes, in fact they say I'm very good at spinning,' said Murra.

'Good, you're hired, come in,' said the farmer's wife, looking delighted. 'I'm fed up with working so hard. I can leave you to do the work, and I'm going into town to the fair.' She put on her best bonnet as if she couldn't wait a minute more.

'All this carded fleece here is to be spun, Murra,' she said, waving at five large sacks of creamy-white fleece. 'The weaver's coming to collect the wool tomorrow, so be sure that you finish it by the time I get home at nightfall – or there'll be hell to pay!'

The farmer's wife flounced out of the door to her carriage. Murra looked at the sacks of fleece in despair.

'There must be four full days' work here,' she thought. 'I'll barely manage a quarter of it. But if I don't do it, she'll make sure I never find work again. What am I to do?'

Murra span, and span, all that morning, so fast that her fingers were bleeding and her mind was racing. By lunchtime she was scarcely halfway into the first sack of fleece. It was no good, she would never get it done.

So Murra stopped spinning and went over to the kitchen window, and through a blur of tears she looked out at an old hawthorn tree in the garden, all twisted-trunked and lichen-covered. Its strong green leaves were twirling around as if they were dancing – even though it was a fine still day with no wind. The leaves of the elder tree and the rowan tree were doing the same thing.

'Perhaps the Good People are here today,' she thought. 'Could they help me? After all, I have been their friend, and always remembered them.'

She went out into the noontime sunshine of the garden and told her woes to the elder and to the rowan. Then she took off her boots and stockings, went to the hawthorn and started to walk around the tree, her bare feet treading quietly but firmly in the grass, moving clockwise as the old stories said. 'Good People, I need your help with my spinning. Please help me!' she repeated over and over.

Murra circled the thorn tree once, twice, three times, repeating her words over and over. There was no reply. She kept going. Four, five, six times … Still nothing.

On the seventh time, just as her bare feet completed the circle, a gruff little voice spoke, 'I know where the Good People are! I can find them for you, Murra!'

There was a rustling noise, and the elder tree and rowan tree started to shake; and then a hairy, ugly little man tumbled out of the trees, grinning all over.

This must be the Fenoderee! Murra quickly curtsied to him.

'We know you, Murra,' said the little man, and his black eyes twinkled. 'You're a good girl. Now, I suggest you do exactly what I say. Go back to the kitchen, throw open the door to the garden, and say clearly and loudly, "All welcomes on you, magic spinners!" After that, go away from here! Go for a nice walk until the evening falls and the moon is rising over the mountains, and then you must return to the kitchen. But – this is very important – before you go back in, knock on the door, open it and say, "All blessings on you, magic spinners!" Then, you shall see what they have done to help.'

And with that, the Fenoderee bowed low and disappeared.

So Murra went back to the kitchen and flung open the kitchen door to the summer sunshine. 'All welcomes on you, magic spinners!' she cried to the garden. There was no reply, but Murra didn't wait to find out more: she went for a long walk, all through the heaths out to the coast, and back round again through the trees. When the darkness fell and the bright sickle moon began to rise over the mountains, she turned around and went back to the farmhouse.

The door was closed, but as she got closer Murra could hear clicks and whirrs and high-pitched songs going on inside. She walked round the house and tried to peep through the window, but it had been covered by a cloudy white curtain and Murra couldn't see inside. So she went back to the kitchen door, gathered up all her courage, knocked on the door, and flung it open.

The kitchen was full of tiny people, each no higher than Murra's knee. They were dressed in bright colours: a red cap here, a yellow jacket there, striped stockings; and each was sitting in front of a miniature spinning wheel, spinning so quickly both the wheels and the fingers of the Good People were a blur. In the middle of the kitchen, on the table, was a heap of woollen skeins of many different patterns – there must have been hundreds of them, and more were being thrown into the centre from the spinners as she watched.

'All blessings on you, magic spinners!' cried Murra.

Immediately the Good People all leapt up and the wheels whirred to a stop. They threw their last skeins of wool on to the table, hoisted their spinning wheels onto their shoulders and, without a single word, they filed out of the kitchen door past Murra, into the moonlight and away.

All that was left in the kitchen was the huge pile of woollen yarn on the table. The sacks of fleece were gone.

Murra walked back into the kitchen and sat down, dazed. She had only been there a few minutes when there was a clatter of cartwheels in the yard, and the farmer's wife came home, a little the worse for wear and smelling of drink. She was astonished, and not a little annoyed, to see the skeins of wool on the table, because she had known the task she'd set for Murra was impossible.

The farmer's wife peered closer at the wool. 'It's all spun into funny patterns!' she cried. 'Don't try to tell me this is your own work. You've been messing with Them, haven't you?'

Murra's cheeks flushed. 'Yes, they have helped me ... But haven't they done their work beautifully? I have never seen anything like it. And they didn't do any harm.'

'Is that right?' said the farmer's wife. 'Then what's that all over my kitchen window?' She walked, slightly unsteadily, towards the cloudy film over the window and tried to snatch it away, but it was stuck fast, like a thick mat of cobweb. 'Clean away this stuff immediately, or you'll be for it!'

Murra walked over to the window and reached up to the fairy curtain. As soon as she touched it, the fabric fell away into her hands, shimmering and light. It was a shawl, sparkling with the colours of a thousand wild flowers: primrose, harebell, tormentil, bell heather, may blossom, scabious, lady's bedstraw, ivy ... all gleaming with light as if they had been touched with the first rays of the sun at dawn. It was a fairy shawl, and Murra knew that it was meant for her.

'Give that here!' The farmer's wife snatched up the shawl and draped it around herself, but as soon as she touched it the fabric turned to ashen grey, and as she walked forward it fell off her shoulders. Again and again she tried to put it back, but it wouldn't stay wrapped around her.

'It's a curse!' screamed the farmer's wife. 'Take it out of my kitchen and get out! I'll not have fairy folks in MY house!'

Murra quietly put the shawl around her own shoulders, where it stayed, shimmering again with all the flowers of the wild. Then she walked out of that kitchen door for the last time, and never went back. Murra knew that gifts from the Good People were precious; and so good luck and happiness were hers, all the days that she lived.

Yallery Brown

Dandelions are loud, and bright, and they are everywhere. Particularly in the springtime, their yellow flowers carpet the countryside in all kinds of conditions, and dandelion seedheads are a favourite way for children to tell the time.

But dandelions are also tenacious, and any gardener will tell you it's nearly impossible to get rid of a dandelion's tap root once it has taken hold. This story from Lincolnshire tells of an altogether unpleasant flower fairy. Or is he?

Tom was only a lad at the time, he couldn't have been more than eighteen, and he worked at the big farm at the edge of the village. It was a long walk along the road to the farm and back from where Tom lived, and so he used to take a short cut across the fields, and nobody seemed to mind.

One night, Tom was walking back from the farm by his usual short cut. It was a mild night in late spring, and Tom was in a cider haze – he didn't have a care in the world. The air was still and the full moon was bright behind him, casting shadows of his figure and of all the dandelion clocks dotted across the grass. Tom smiled to himself and muttered, 'Well, if I need to heed the time, now, this would be a good place! But I don't much care what time it is.'

The night was full of little sounds as though the trees and the grass and the flowers and the insects were chattering to themselves. And all at once there was a louder noise ahead of him. It was a pitiful, heartbroken sob, followed by a high-pitched wailing and a painful catching of breath, like a small child all taken up with fear. It made Tom feel sick to hear it.

He began to look everywhere for the poor thing. 'It must be Sally Bratton's child,' he thought to himself; she was always doing other things than being a proper mother. But though he looked and looked, he couldn't see where the noise was coming from. It was getting louder, and he thought he could make out some words:

'Ooh, the stone, the great big stone! Ooh! The stone on top!'

Naturally Tom wondered where the stone might be, and he looked again, and there at the bottom of the hedge close by was a great flat stone, half-buried in the grass and earth. Tom knelt down and put his ear to the stone, and there was the little sobbing voice, clearer than ever: 'Ooh! Ooh, the stone, the stone on top!'

Tom couldn't bear the pitiful noise, and so he tore at the stone until he felt it lifting out from the mat of grass and damp earth that held it. He tugged some more and all at once the stone came free and toppled him backwards. The wailing stopped, and Tom got up from his fall and went back to where the stone had been.

And there in the hole lay a tiddy thing on its back, blinking up at the moon and at him. It was no bigger than a year-old baby, but it had long hair and a beard twisted all around its body so that you couldn't see its clothes; and the hair was all yellow and shining and silky and downy like a child's. But the face of the tiddy thing was ancient, just a heap of wrinkles, as if it had been hundreds of years since the skin was taut and smooth. Its hands and feet were brown, the colour of the fresh-turned earth in the spring, and two bright black beady eyes peered up at Tom from a brown, tear-stained face, grimacing at the bright moonlight.

The creature's eyes got used to the moonlight in time, and his face became bolder. 'Tom,' he said, 'you're a good lad!' His voice was high and piping like a scolding little bird. 'You're a good lad?' The voice took on a questioning tone.

Tom touched his hat and looked for a coin in his pocket to turn over, and began to think what he ought to say. But the tiddy thing carried on. 'Oh, Tom, Tom, you've no need to be afraid of me – you have done me a better turn than you know, and now I can do the same for you!' Tom was still too scared to speak, but he thought to himself, 'Lord! For sure – it's a bogle!'

'No!' said the little man, quick as quick, 'I am no bogle, but you'd better not ask what I am; anyway I'm a good friend of yours.'

It could read his thoughts! Tom had better show this little thing some respect.

'Might I know your honour's name?'

'H'm,' the tiddy thing pulled at his yellow beard in thought at that. 'Yes. That's it. Yallery Brown you can call me, Yallery

Brown – it's my nature, you see, and it'll do as well as any other for a name. Yallery Brown's your friend, Tom. And now, I'm in a hurry tonight, but tell me quick, what shall I do for you? Would you have a bonny wife? Or, as much gold as you can carry? Or will you have help with something else? Just say the word, and it will happen.'

Tom scratched his head. 'Well, I've no hankering after a wife, that's for sure, that would be nothing but trouble; and gold doesn't worry me; but as for work? Well, I can't be having with it – work is just too much bother if you ask me. So if you could do all the work for me, I'd thank –'

'Stop,' said Yallery Brown, quick as lightning, 'I'll help you and welcome, but if you ever say that to me – if you ever thank me, you'll never see me again. I WANT no thanks, I'll HAVE no thanks!' And he stamped his little foot on the earth as if the very idea of thanks was enough to send him into a rage.

'Remember that now, you great lump, Tom,' he went on, calming down a bit, 'and if you ever need help, or get into trouble, call on me and just say, "Yallery Brown, come up from the earth, I want you!" and I'll be with you at once. And now,' he said, picking a dandelion clock, 'good night to you,' and he blew on the dandelion clock, and Tom's eyes and ears were clouded with fine white dandelion down, as if a mist had fallen. As soon as he could see again, Yallery Brown was gone; and if it hadn't been for the upturned stone and the hole in the earth at his feet, he would have thought he'd been dreaming.

Well, Tom went home and to bed; and by the morning he'd forgotten all about it. But when he went to the farm, there was no work to do! All was done already, the horses seen to, the stables cleaned out, everything in its proper place, and he'd nothing to do but sit around. And so it went on day after day, all Tom's work done by Yallery Brown, and better done, too, than Tom would have done it himself. And if Tom was given more work, he sat down, and the work did itself, the hay stooks piling high, or the broom sweeping. Tom never saw Yallery Brown in daylight; it was only in the dusk he saw him hopping about, like a Will-o-the-wisp without his lantern.

At first this all worked out very well for Tom; he'd no work to do, and good pay for it as well; but by and by, things started to go wrong. If the work was done for Tom, it was undone for all the other lads on the farm. If Tom's buckets were filled, theirs were upset; if his tools were sharpened, theirs were blunted and spoiled; if his horses were clean, theirs were splashed with muck, and so on. The lads saw Yallery Brown flitting around in the dusk, and they saw all Tom's work getting done by invisible hands, day in, day out. And gradually the lads wouldn't talk to Tom, they wouldn't come near him, they would tease him and tell tales to their master about him, and so things went from bad to worse. Tom's anxiety and his worry started to grow on him like a weed.

Tom decided that it would be best to start working properly at the farm again, so that Yallery Brown would leave him alone; but he found that he could do nothing himself, even if he chose to. The brooms wouldn't stay in his hand, the plough ran away from him, the hoe kept falling out of his grip. He could only sit by and look on, and have the cold shoulder turned on him, while Yallery Brown was making life difficult for the others, and working for him.

At last, things got so bad that the master gave Tom the sack, and if he hadn't, all the rest of the lads would have made it impossible for him to stay at the farm. Naturally,

Tom felt bad; it was a very good place, and good pay too. So Tom went out into the same field, all yellow with dandelions, where he had first found Yallery Brown, and he shook his fist in the air and called out as loud as he could, 'Yallery Brown, come from the earth; you scamp, I want you here, you are nothing but trouble to me!'

Tom had hardly shouted the words when something was pinching the back of his right knee, making him jump; and when he turned and looked down, there was the tiny figure of Yallery Brown, swathed in bright yellow shining hair, his wrinkled face curled up in a huge grin and his glinting black eyes laughing at Tom.

Tom would have liked to have kicked him, but there was scarcely enough to get his boot against; so he said, 'Look here, I'll thank you kindly to leave me alone after this, do you hear? I want none of your help, and I'll have no more to do with you!'

The tiddy man broke into a screeching laugh, and pointed his brown finger at Tom. 'Ho, ho, Tom!' he said. 'You've thanked me, my lad, and I told you not to, I told you not to!'

'I never want to see you again. Get out of here!' shouted Tom, exasperated.

Yallery Brown only laughed and screeched and danced and mocked, as long as Tom went on swearing, but eventually he calmed down a little – and then Yallery Brown spoke.

'Tom, my lad,' he said with a grin, 'I'll tell you something important, Tom. True, I'll never help you again, and call as much as you like, you will never see me after today. But I never said that I'd leave you alone, Tom, and I never will! I was nice and safe under the stone, Tom, and I could do no harm; but you let me out yourself, and you can't put me back again! I would have been your friend and worked for you, if you had been wise; but since you're no more than a plain fool, I'll give you no more than a born fool's luck. When it all goes wrong for you, Tom, you'll know that it's Yallery Brown's doing, even though you don't see him. Remember my words!'

And Yallery Brown began to sing, dancing around Tom, like a baby with his yellow hair, but looking older than ever with his grinning wrinkled brown bit of a face:

Work as you will, you'll never do well;
Work as you might, you'll never gain favour;
For harm and mischief and Yallery Brown
You've let them all out from under the stone.

Tom could never really remember what Yallery Brown said next – it was all cursing and calling down misfortune on him, and all Tom could do was stare in horror. But eventually, the yellow shining hair of Yallery Brown rose up into the air in

a miniature whirlwind, and wrapped itself around the tiny figure until he looked for all the world like a great dandelion clock; and the clock floated away on the wind over the hedge and out of sight, with a little wicked laugh by way of parting.

And did it come true? It surely did. Tom worked here and there, and turned his hand to this and that, but it always went awry, and he could never settle. He married a woman he didn't love, who was nothing but trouble for him, and all their children died, but his wife didn't; and the crops rotted in the fields, and the beasts never fattened properly, and nothing ever did well for Tom. Always, right through to his final days, Yallery Brown's voice was in Tom's ear:

Work as you will, you'll never do well;
Work as you might, you'll never gain favour;
For harm and mischief and Yallery Brown
You've let them all out from under the stone.

THE FIELD

I first heard Nick Hennessey tell this story, many years ago, and since then I've heard versions by other tellers. Here's mine. It shows how the very existence of wild plants in the countryside is beholden to those people who own and manage the land, and asks: what do they really care about?

There is a field, somewhere in the middle of Devon, near a very big river. It's one of thousands and thousands of fields, but this particular field is very special (I'm not going to tell you exactly where it is, because that's secret).

In fact, before it was a field, and way back when Devon was called Dumnonia, this was one of the places that King Arthur and his knights travelled through on their way between Tintagel and Glastonbury. The centuries rolled on, trees were cleared, and fields tilled, and about six hundred years ago hedgebanks were created to make this land into a field.

But since that time, the original rights to this little parcel of Devon have been forgotten. Even after the two world wars and 'Dig for Victory', even after the last agricultural revolution, nobody has successfully laid claim to this field, and nobody is quite sure who owns it, even the Land Registry; and because it is away from roads and public footpaths, there are very few people who know about it. It's as if time has stood still in this field: someone must graze animals on it occasionally, because it is still a wildflower meadow, and it's stayed much the same for centuries.

There is a farm on one side of the field, sloping down to the river. On this farm, all the fields are small and the hedges have been laid traditionally, and they are alive and full of catkins in the springtime, and birds busy nesting, and tall oak and ash trees thinking about coming into leaf. There are long grass margins by the hedges full of stitchwort, and fields of clover and hay-grass; there are other fields cultivated through organic methods; there are traditional Devon Red cattle, classic tractors in the yard, and chickens pecking about.

And the owner of this farm – called Oak Farm – is absolutely sure that he owns the field.

There is a farm on the other side of the field, sloping down to the river. This is what a modern farmer would call a 'good, productive farm'. Every single field is bright green with monoculture productive grass strains, courtesy of the Agritech companies, and some have recently been re-sown, and ploughed right up to the edges of the hedgerows. The hedges themselves have been flailed to within a couple of inches of the hedgebank, at least twice last year – they are nearly lifeless, but they are neat and tidy and straight-edged. There are black and white dairy cows in a huge concreted yard, with a slurry store full to overflowing with the brown stuff.

And the owner of this farm – called Ash Farm – is convinced that he owns the field.

In fact, you probably won't be surprised to hear that these two farmers really hate each other, and each of them has tried a number of ways to prove that he owns that field, legal or otherwise, and neither of them has dared to do anything much with the land in the meantime. They haven't spoken for years, probably even decades, although each of them owns a fine pair of binoculars and keeps an eye on each other's business and they both pretend that they don't.

Now you know all about the field, the story can begin.

One day last June, around late afternoon, Farmer Oak decided to go out for a walk on his field – or the field he believed was his field. He squelched in his wellies through the soggy bits, and admired the pink of the ragged robin flowers and marsh orchids and the marsh fritillary butterflies that flitted about, and wandered up the slope to the drier part of the field which was already yellow with trefoil. Over the brow he went, and it was there that he nearly ran straight into Farmer Ash, who had decided it was such a nice afternoon he would go for a wander in his field – or the field he believed was his field.

Farmer Oak looked Farmer Ash straight in the eye and uttered the time-honoured words: 'Get off my land!'

'What do you mean, YOUR land?' said Farmer Ash. 'This is my field and you know it full well. Go on, clear off.'

'YOUR field?' said Farmer Oak. 'You wouldn't know the value of the place even if you DID own it. Did you know this is one of the last remaining fields of wildflower grassland in the whole of Devon?'

'Oh VERY nice,' said Farmer Ash. 'The problem with you nature-folks is that you don't live in the real world. This is wasteland! I can't put my dairy herd on here! What it needs, of course, is decent drainage and a good load of fertiliser, then it might be useable.'

'Just as well that I own it, then,' said Farmer Oak. 'I'll be able to keep it safe from vandals like you, who call yourself farmers. You care absolutely nothing for the place, do you? I've seen you tipping slurry into the river when you think nobody's looking. I've seen you load chemicals on your fields, year after year. That's the problem with you modern farmers, you take the public subsidy like it's your birthright, then you screw the place to within an inch of its life, all in the name of profit. Well, you're not going to do it here.'

They were shouting now. 'For your information,' said Farmer Ash. 'That's right, I am a REAL farmer, and I grow food, you know, to feed people. Farming is an industry, and right now the supermarkets have got us by the balls on milk prices. I can't afford to worry about pretty flowers and babbling rivers. I live in the *real* world in the twenty-first century. We don't need organic yogurt-knitting comer-inners like you. I'm telling you for the last time – get off my land!'

I can't tell you who threw the first punch, but I can tell you that they got into a big fight in the middle of that field. It wasn't very pretty. And it wasn't long before the fighting turned into wrestling, getting nearer and nearer to the river; and it wasn't long after that, that Farmer Oak found himself standing with his hands locked around Farmer Ash's throat, and Farmer Ash found himself with his hands locked around Farmer Oak's throat.

They were stuck, staring each other in the face, growling at one another. Neither of them would move, for fear of the other gaining advantage.

An hour went past. They were still there, hands around each other's throats. Another hour passed. It was getting dark now. Still there.

They stayed there all night in the field, Farmer Oak with his hands round Farmer Ash's throat, Farmer Ash with his hands round Farmer Oak's throat. There was little sound in the middle of the night – a few owls hooting to each other, the sound of the never-ending river.

Dawn started to show, a fine, clear morning. They were still there, with dew forming all over them. The first birds started singing – well, only over Farmer Oak's farm, of course, there weren't many on Farmer Ash's land. The first skylark rose up into the dawn and started its song. A woodpecker started laughing.

They were still there, hands around each other's throats.

Then they both heard a different sound. It was the sound of squelching mud, and it was coming towards them. Neither dared to look round, in case the other one got the advantage.

The squelching noise came closer, and then it stopped. What was it?

'I'm not looking. I don't trust you,' said Farmer Oak.

'I'm not turning my head neither,' said Farmer Ash.

'Tell you what. Why don't we both turn our heads at the same time. One ... two ... three.'

They both turned to look, and standing next to them, peering up at them, was a little old lady, in wellies far too big for her.

'What on earth are you two doing?' she said.

'He's on my land and he refused to leave,' said Farmer Oak.

'What do you mean, YOUR land? This land belongs to me!' cried Farmer Ash.

They started fighting again.

The little old lady said nothing, but she got down on her hands and knees in the mud and put her head against the ground, turned to one side. Then she muttered. Then she nodded.

Both the farmers were curious now. 'What on earth are YOU doing?' they said.

'Well,' said the little old lady, getting up and wiping the mud off her hands. 'I've asked the land for its opinion. And the land says that *you* belong to *it*.'

And what happened after that? What do you think?

THE TULIP PIXIES

There's something peculiarly obsessive about the English and their gardens, and I like to think that it reflects a deep love of the land, and the need to work with it.

Tulips weren't recorded in Britain before the sixteenth century, and they became so highly prized in the seventeenth century that 'tulip mania' developed. I love the other old-fashioned garden plants in this story: the single rose, the cornflower (blue-buttons), the wallflower, stocks or pinks (all called gillyflower), forget-me-nots, and rue or 'Herb of Grace', brought here by the Romans as a medicinal plant. Parsley used to be called the 'Herb of Death' and Devon folklore says that anyone who transplants parsley will offend the 'guardian genius' who presides over parsley beds.

In the West Country, down near the river Tavy, a kind old woman once lived in a little cottage. She lived near a piskie field, and you could see the green piskie rings in the grass. Some people said that the piskie rings were caused by the piskies catching Dartmoor ponies, and riding round and round in circles on the grass in the dead of night. But the old woman knew that wasn't the reason why the piskie rings were there.

Around her little cottage was a pretty garden, full of sweet-smelling flowers. It was the kind of garden that looked effortless and natural, even though she was hard at work outside all the seasons round. The gardening work paid off. Lavender and hollyhocks grew there and were glad, lilies and rosemary and the sweetbriar tree, blue-buttons and gillyflowers, forget-me-nots and rue. But the old woman's pride and joy was a big bed of bright red tulips, and she took great care to look after it. Everyone stopped in the road to peep over her gate when the time of tulips came.

It wasn't only passers-by that enjoyed the place. The piskies liked the kind old woman, and they liked her garden too.

One starry spring night, as she lay asleep, with the scented lilac flowers under her window, she woke up to a strange sound. At first she thought it was an owl in the elm tree, but gradually, as she became more conscious, she realised this was a much sweeter noise, even a tune. 'It sounds almost like a lullaby,' she thought.

She lay there for a few minutes enjoying the music, and then she got out of bed and looked out of the window. There, below her in the moonlight, all the tulips were waving their shining petals in tune with the sweet music. It seemed like the tulips were singing too.

When the same thing happened the next night, and the next, the old woman began to see what was happening. The piskie folks had brought their babies to the tulip bed, and laid each one within a separate flower.

'They're lulling their little ones to sleep! See – the piskie babies are fast asleep, and there go the piskie folk to dance in the meadow.'

She was right. It wasn't the catching of Dartmoor ponies that made those rings on the green grass, but the dancing of the little folk to the tune of the pipes. But as the dawn started up in the east, back came the piskies to collect their infants from the tulip cradles, where they lay asleep. Then the piskies and their babies started to fade away and become invisible in the new morning light.

'Bless my soul! If they didn't kiss the little dears before they picked them up,' said the old woman. 'How much love is here!'

She noticed that the tulips didn't fade so quickly as the other flowers in the garden, although the rest of the spring flowers had long since gone over. And as she bent to have a look at the tulips, the old woman noticed that they had a delicious fragrance, just the way that tulips could smell if they had a scent. The piskies had made them even lovelier by breathing over them.

'Now, nobody shall pick a single tulip, not even myself,' said the old woman. 'They are for the piskies.'

And so it went on, year after year.

But sadly, one spring day the old woman died. The tulips hung their heads in grief, as well they might, for it wasn't long before the garden passed into other hands.

The new owner didn't care about piskies. All he cared about was growing food that he could eat, and food that he could sell. The garden started to be taken over by gooseberry bushes, raspberry canes, greengages and plum trees.

'You shouldn't gather all of the gooseberries, leave some for the piskies,' warned the man's neighbour, 'otherwise it's proper unlucky. The piskies won't stand for being robbed of their own.'

'Piskies? Don't be ridiculous!' said the man.

'You're not thinking of digging up those tulips?' said another. 'Those were the old woman's special flowers, those ones. What are you replacing them with?'

'I'm setting a bed of parsley, if you must know,' said the man.

'Parsley! Dear God! Don't you know it's mortal unlucky to set parsley? Last man I heard of who did that was bedridden for life.'

'Stuff and nonsense!' snapped the new owner of the garden.

So all the magical flowers were grubbed up, and parsley seeds set instead. But they never came up. The piskies were so offended that they wouldn't let anything grow anew, and anything the man had left in the garden just withered away. The whole garden was soon a wasteland of hard, bare ground and struggling weeds. All the man's gardening hopes went hungry.

Although the garden no longer heard the piskie's lullabies, the little folk still sang. But this time the singing came from the old woman's grave. The tune was sad and sorrowful, and it was always sung the night before the moon was properly full.

Nobody bothered to tend the old woman's grave, and yet not a single weed could be seen on it. As she had tended the tulip bed, now the little people tended her grave. Nobody was ever seen to plant a flower, but somehow her favourites sprang up in the night – lilies and rosemary, blue-buttons and gillyflowers, forget-me-nots and rue, and bright red tulips, all growing gladly.

5

The Height of the Green

Summer tree, winter tree
Bunch of flowers, now there's showers.
Game with summer grasses, Buckinghamshire

It's midsummer and the sun is at its height. Most green growth is now done, in preparation for the ripening to come. This is the time of greatest energy, most busyness, as the year and the plant world is at its peak. Time to enjoy some midsummer madness, although the effects will follow soon after …

THE JUNIPER TREE

*Together with yew and Scots pine, juniper is one of only three
native conifers in Britain and Ireland. The charity Plantlife
considers that it may be extinct in lowland England over the
next fifty years, if conservation action is not taken.*

*In Ireland and Scotland, juniper was used as protection
against evil forces. Never tell a secret under a juniper tree
because they are gossips, as this cautionary tale clearly demon-
strates. This story comes from Buckinghamshire, and I can just
see the landscape around the Chiltern hills: windmill, chalk soil,
thyme, juniper and all.*

There was a mill beneath a steep chalk down. On the
down, many juniper bushes grew: squat, spiky and bearing
dark berries, the juniper bushes were dotted all over the
bare hillside.

Not much happened in that place, and nobody came by.
Junipers are gossips, nearly as bad as pine trees, and they get
bored very easily. In this quiet, chalky place, the older juniper
bushes were so bored that they started to die out from their
middles and collapse in desperation.

The only people the juniper bushes ever saw brought their
corn in carts along the track down by the river. The junipers
gossiped about them constantly, and thought how nice it
would be if they did something interesting.

Then it happened. One day, a man crept over the down
with a sack of stolen corn on his back. He tiptoed past the
juniper bushes, offered the stolen corn to the miller, and the
miller welcomed him as if he had known all along.

Soon, every juniper for miles knew all about it too. They
were so excited that in only a few hours, the village constable

also heard, and he brought others along with him to that lonely place, to arrest the robbers.

The thief and the miller were tried and convicted. And that gave the junipers even more to gossip about.

THE LEGEND OF KNOCKGRAFTON

Foxgloves make a spectacular purple show at the beginning of the summer. One old name for foxglove is 'fairy-bell' and another is 'lusmore'.

In County Leitrim, the old advice to tell whether you had a changeling, or simply a disagreeable human child, was to squeeze the juice of the foxglove on the child and then to swing the child three times out the door on a shovel, saying 'If you're a fairy away with you!' Apparently the fairy children would die, while the human ones would become better behaved! Modern medicine, in contrast, uses digitalis from foxgloves as a heart medicine (in tiny concentrations due to the high toxicity of the juice).

This story has very old versions from Scotland and England, as well as this version from the south of Ireland. Fiacha was the name of a number of high kings of Ireland.

A poor man once lived in the fertile glen of Aherlow, at the foot of the Galtee mountains. He had a great hump on his back, and looked for all the world as if his body had been rolled up and placed upon his shoulders. The hump was a great weight on his frame that forced him to look at the ground as he walked.

The man's name was Lusmore, after the fairy-bell foxglove that he always used to wear in his cap for protection. And protection he needed; for although he was as harmless and inoffensive as a man could be, the country people around had made up stories about him. They said Lusmore knew a lot about herb-lore and charms, and you should be afraid to meet him on a dark night, which was very unfair. But he did have a great skill, of straw-plaiting and straw-weaving, and maybe that is why some jealous people had started the stories.

One early summer evening Lusmore was returning home to Cappagh, and as he couldn't help but walk slowly, it took him a lot longer than anyone else. It was quite dark when he came to the old burial mound of Knockgrafton alongside the road. Lusmore was tired, and he decided that here was as good a place as any to rest for the night.

Knockgrafton had a well-known ancient well, where Fiacha had placed silver cups for anyone wishing to drink, to offer hospitality and show his rule of law. Sure enough, Lusmore found the well and a silver cup, drank his fill of the cool, clear water, and gave his thanks to the ancients and to the guardians of the place.

He sat with his humped back against the grassy bank, and looked mournfully up to the moon. She was full and round, casting her ghostly light across the grass and picking out the bells of the foxgloves that grew all around him.

After a little while, Lusmore thought that he could hear music. This wasn't any kind of music he had heard before; it was high and rich and full of harmony, many voices rising on the night air and blending effortlessly with the lilt of the words. Soon he could hear the words:

Monday, Tuesday, Monday, Tuesday, Monday, Tuesday …

After three rounds there would be a moment's pause, and then it would start again, just the same.

Lusmore listened carefully, scarcely daring to breathe in case he missed a note. The singing was coming from the moat. Although it was charming, eventually even the patient Lusmore began to get tired of the same simple round, sung over, and over, and over again. So, he waited for the pause in the singing, and when it arrived he sang the same tune, but with different words:

And Wednesday too …

And then he carried on singing the same round as the other voices, finishing the melody, on the pause again, with:

And Wednesday too …

The round was being sung by fairies, and when they heard Lusmore's tuneful, timely addition to their song they were delighted. Lusmore was lifted up and travelling at speed through the burial mound to what lay beneath – the land of fairies.

Lusmore found himself dancing with the little people, twirling round and round and round with a curious lightness, to the sweetest music that kept time for the dancing. He was made welcome with fine food and drink, and ate to his heart's content, being sure to thank everyone as he went.

Presently one of the fairies called for quiet, and said:

Lusmore, Lusmore!
Despair not, nor deplore,
For the hump which you bore

On your back is no more;
Look down on the floor
And see it, Lusmore!

As soon as these words were said, Lusmore felt himself so light, and so happy, that he thought he could have bounded at one jump over the moon. He saw his hump tumble down upon the ground from his shoulders. He then tried to lift up his head, worried that he might hit the ceiling of the great fairy hall where he stood, and this caused much good-natured hilarity among the fairies. For the first time in his life, he could stand straight; he turned round and round again, and everything appeared more and more beautiful; and Lusmore became so overwhelmed that he passed out.

When Lusmore woke, it was broad daylight, with the sun shining brightly and the larks high in the sky. He was sitting with his back against the bank at the edge of the Knockgrafton mound, with foxgloves all around him, and cows grazing peacefully nearby.

Lusmore felt between his shoulder blades for the hump, but there was nothing there. His spine was as straight and true as he had always dreamed. But it was real. And he was wearing a full suit of new clothes, which he could only suppose the fairies had made for him.

'Thank you, fairies! Thank you a million times!' said Lusmore. He plucked a foxglove stem covered in purple fairy bells, and fixed it into his new cap.

He skipped towards Cappagh, taking each step lightly and happily. When he got back home, he had great difficulty persuading everyone that he was the same man – for, at least as far as outward appearances went, he wasn't. He carried on his straw-plaiting, and he started dancing as well, and none with a broader smile than Lusmore.

It wasn't long before Lusmore's story was the talk of the countryside, for miles around. It wasn't long after that when Lusmore was visited by an old woman, who asked to speak to him urgently.

'I hear that you had your hump taken off by the fairies? The only son of a friend of mine has got a hump on him that will be his death. Maybe, if he used the same charm as you, he could be cured. Can you tell me more about the charm and how it worked?'

Lusmore was good-natured and generous, and so he told the old woman how he had added to the tune for the fairies at Knockgrafton and how his hump had been taken from his shoulders, and how he had got a suit of new clothes into the bargain.

The woman thanked him very much, and then went away to her friend and told her everything. The hump-backed son of her friend was called Jack Madden. He had always been a bad-tempered and cunning young man, who believed more in tricking people by his own wit, than by any protection or charms; but after some persuasion, Jack set off for Knockgrafton with his mother and the old woman. He was left alone, sitting expectantly with his back against the bank of the old burial mound, just before nightfall. They knew nothing of any wells or silver cups.

Jack hadn't been sitting there long when he heard the tune going on within the moat. He didn't know, but it was much sweeter than before; for the fairies were singing it the way Lusmore had settled their music for them, and the round repeated without a pause:

Monday, Tuesday, Monday, Tuesday, Monday, Tuesday, and Wednesday too …

Jack Madden, who was in a great hurry to be rid of his hump, never thought of waiting for the fairies to pause, or about whether his tune would harmonise with the rest. So at a random point in the round, he suddenly yelled out:

And Thursday too!

No sooner had the words passed his lips than he was taken up and whisked into the burial mound by the fairies, who crowded round him with angry faces, screeching and scream-ing, 'Who spoiled our tune? Who spoiled our tune?' One stepped up to him and said:

Jack Madden! Jack Madden!
Your words sound so bad in
The tune we feel glad in;
This place that you stand in,
That your life we may sadden;
Here's two humps for Jack Madden!

And twenty of the strongest fairies brought Lusmore's hump and put it down on Jack's back, over his own, where it became fixed as firmly as if it were nailed on. Out of their land under the hill, and in the morning when Jack's mother and her friend came to look after him, they found him half dead, lying against the grassy bank, with the two humps upon his back.

Home they all went, horrified; and through the weight of his other hump, and the long journey, Jack Madden died soon after, leaving his heavy curse to anyone who would go to listen to fairy tunes again.

JACK AND THE BEANSTALK

Recent studies suggest that this story, one of the most well known of our native folk tales, is over five thousand years old. It set me to thinking – not only about runner beans (one of my favourite foods) but also about what's actually happening in this story. It's pretty violent and disgusting in places, and our hero Jack is a thief. What is he really stealing, and what is he learning? And what's the giant doing at the top of the beanstalk – who is he, and who is his mother? Here's my own version, with a different perspective from most.

This is an ancient story, even though it only happened last year.

It's about a piece of England, dark soil and hard-worked ground, land curving out to the horizon. Many living things used to thrive in that place, but now only one plant lived there, and that was wheat.

Row upon row upon huge square field of rows of wheat, bright luscious green in the spring, golden and uniform in the summer, sprayed with chemicals to kill off any other plant that dared to try growing there, and then scythed to the ground by giant machines driven by tiny men. Then the whole thing started again for the next year with machines and more sacks of chemicals. Those who milled the wheat, transported it, made it into bread, and eventually ate it, hardly spared a thought for where it had grown.

The wheat giant went on and on, stamping his mark all over miles of this place, apart from one tiny patch, close to a little town, but far away enough to be called countryside. In the corner of this little patch of green was a run-down cottage. There were rows of vegetables in the garden, bean canes and pea sticks and potato rows. There were broken-down fruit cages going rotten. There was an empty chicken coop, and there was a slightly forlorn brown cow, making the most of the rest of the field. And there, in the vegetable garden, was a woman weeding and digging, puffing and sighing as she went.

Oh, it had all seemed like a great idea to start with, the Good Life. It was honest and hardworking and back to the soil; it got out of the rat race; it meant something. But then her husband had fallen ill, and after she had spent a year looking after him he had died, leaving her and her son to carry on alone.

That was five years ago, and her son, Jack, had never lifted a finger to help his mother out in that whole time. Well, he was a teenage boy, what did she expect? He would come around, he just needed some time. He was a good lad at heart. Things would get better. They had to.

But Jack had no interest in helping his mother out with the housework or the plot. There he was, in his bedroom, playing computer games, and wasting time in other ways that only teenagers fully appreciate; and when he wasn't in his room he was out with the lads, going into town, getting bored, winding people up. It was easy to be lazy and careless when you were Jack, but quite difficult to be extravagant, because they had nothing – and yet Jack managed it, somehow.

The upshot of this sorry situation was that, one by one, their possessions had to be sold to buy food and clothes and pay off debt – until all they had left, apart from the little cottage and the bit of land they lived on, was the cow. It was the last link with the Good Life.

Jack ambled home from not doing very much in particular one day, and his mother met him at the door with tears in her eyes. For the first time in her life, she told him off. 'Jack, you've never done anything to help, and here's me slaving for a few pennies here and there and having to sell everything we possess; and now, we have no food, and all I can do is sell the cow. I am so sad to let her go; but there is nothing else for it.'

For about five minutes Jack felt a bit guilty, but it was soon over, and he offered to help by selling the cow for his mother at the market in the town the next morning. 'Make sure you get a good price for her,' said his mother.

'This'll be a laugh,' thought Jack. Off he went the next morning, and yet he couldn't help feeling a bit embarrassed leading a cow down the lane. 'I hope none of my mates see me.' The cow looked at Jack mournfully as he tugged at the rope. 'Come on, girl. We're going to get you turned into pet food. But you can't understand me, can you? Ha!'

It was a sunny spring morning, and Jack ambled along with the cow on a rope, until he came to a fork in the little lane. Was this the right road? He couldn't remember there being a fork in the road before. Which way to take? It was a Saturday morning, after all, and all possibilities were open. Jack took the left fork, just because it wasn't right.

There were footsteps coming down the lane towards him. 'Oh God, don't let me know them,' thought Jack. But he didn't know this fellow. He was quite tubby, with a butcher's apron and a big grin.

'Hallo, Jack!' said the man. How did this man know his name? He had never seen him before.

'Where are you going with that lovely cow?' And the man scratched the head of the cow, who sidled up to him gratefully.

'I'm taking her to market to sell her for a good price. Have you any idea of the price I might get?' said Jack.

'Well … to be honest, not much for a cow like that, not these days, when people don't know the value of things,' said the man. 'I've got something a lot better to exchange for that cow though, Jack; something much more valuable than boring old money; something I think you'll like, a lad of your … discerning taste.' The man's eyes were twinkling, and out of his pocket he brought a handful of …

Beans.

Jack peered at the beans. They were all different colours; green and red and turquoise and gold. As he looked closer he couldn't see any marks or symbols on them; and the man was winking at him.

'I know what you're thinking; but no, Jack, you'd get into real trouble if you swallowed these. These are magic beans. Plant them in the ground, and see what happens. They'll grow you a ladder to heaven itself. Trust me. You won't be disappointed.'

Jack was excited. You didn't meet this kind of man around the country lanes very often. But he also thought about the money he needed to get for his mother, because she was right – Jack was, after all, a lad with a good heart.

'How do I know you're telling the truth?' he said, eyeing the man suspiciously.

The man started laughing. 'Oh, Jack, Jack, Jack. Tell you what. If it doesn't work then you can bring them back here and I'll give you your old cow back. Can't say fairer than that.'

Well, how could Jack refuse an offer like that? Surely he couldn't lose!

'Right. Thank you. Well, good doing business with you!' said Jack, and he handed over the cow and pocketed the beans. And the butcher walked off with the cow, whistling a little tune.

Jack went back home: 'MOTHER!' There she was, on the ground at the back of the house where the cow had been tethered, digging a new vegetable patch. 'What, have you sold the cow already?' she called out. 'How much did you get for her?'

'You'll never guess,' said Jack, grinning.

'No, you don't say. Fifty? Sixty?'

'Better than that,' said Jack. And he explained all about the magic beans, and held them out to show her.

'What, do you think we're living in a fairy tale, and that everything will just turn out for the best?' Jack had never seen his mother in such a temper before. She smacked his hand with the beans and they flew high in the air, scattering in all directions.

Then she sent Jack to his room. Jack thought the same thing that all teenagers think: 'It's not fair,' and 'She doesn't understand me.'

❧

Jack woke up in the morning much too early. A wood pigeon was calling outside, and the blackbird had already started to sing in the sunrise. There was sunlight: but his room was too dark. Something was looming outside the window. Something green.

Jack ran downstairs and outside in his pyjamas. There, over the vegetable patch and in the bit of grass where the poor old cow used to graze, he saw that some of the beans had taken root, and that the man hadn't been lying. Several beanstalks had grown, and twisted and gangled round one another. The stems were thicker than Jack and as he looked up, the beanstalks had grown so high they pierced right through the white clouds dotted across the sky. Massive green leaves sprouted from the beanstalks all the way up, red flowers were already showing and the bees were buzzing and busy.

But just how far did that beanstalk grow?

Jack put a foot on the lowest leaf-stem. It held his weight well. He grabbed the stem and hoisted himself up on to the next, and then the next; and Jack climbed. The beanstalk was like a giant, green, buzzing ladder, and soon his hands were green from bean juice and sore, and he kept peering out from the leaves to see the little cottage on the ground, getting further and further away all the time.

Jack kept climbing for an hour, then for another hour. He got so far, then thought, 'Can I be bothered to go any further?' but then he reasoned that to climb all the way back down again would be even more effort with nothing to show for it; and so he kept climbing. He started to move through clammy damp cloud, and at last the beanstalk started to become thinner and shakier to climb. Just when he thought there was very little beanstalk left, Jack found himself, exhausted, cold, and ravenous, taking a step up to firm ground, and he collapsed in a heap in a new country, on new soil, with a new sky.

Well, there was no mother there to comfort him or tell him off or bring him food or water, and so after a little while Jack began to stir and look around him. Ancient, twisted trees. Tiny saplings struggling for light. This was a woodland, brown and fusty and smelling of earth and rotting leaves and green shade. It didn't feel like a place where humans were in control; it felt like a place where humans could die quite easily. Although he had played computer games about hunters many, many times, Jack had never set foot in a place like this before in his life.

Jack then decided to do something sensible. He tore a strip from his pyjama shirt and tied it to his beanstalk, so that he could find it in among the trees, and it was there flapping in the breeze like a flag. Then he started to walk in one straight direction through the woods: he may as well go forwards as go back, and find some food, now he was here.

Jack walked on as the sun moved lower in the sky. At times the brambles tore at him; occasionally he heard the snuffle of a wild boar and once there was a distant howl that made his blood run cold. But he kept on walking. By the time the sunlight was turning red-gold, he was almost beaten by hunger and thirst.

Then Jack came to a clearing. As the deer scattered in front of him, there, up ahead, was a huge tree, three times as big as all the others, with a trunk as wide as a house. The branches of this tree reached up into the sky further than Jack could see, with each branch bearing leaves of different kinds – fronds of yew, graceful ash, lobed oak, heart-shaped alder, slender willow. There were ribbons tied to the branches and things hanging down – were they fruits, or baubles? At the base of the tree, almost lost in the undergrowth, there was a little door, and in front of it an old, old woman, staring at him.

'Hello,' said Jack to the old woman, 'could you spare some food and water?'

'It's strange to see a human being round here,' said the old woman. 'Or at least, one who is alive and free. Yes, I can help you; but I must warn you, my son is a fierce giant. You had better have your wits about you, if you want to survive.'

'That's a bit overdramatic,' thought Jack; 'poor old dear, she probably doesn't have much of a life around here, so she has to make up stories.' And he agreed, because he was hungry, and it was getting dark.

Jack followed the old woman through the door, inside the trunk of the tree and up a curving flight of massive wooden stairs that went on … and on … surely the tree wasn't this tall? Then they came out into an open space, and now Jack was closer to the branches and the centre of the tree, closer to the life of the thing. It was twilight now and he couldn't see very well, but he could just about make out the shapes of children, teenagers, old men, people of all ages, all bound and hanging upside down by their ankles.

'Ignore them,' said the old woman; 'this is my son's larder. Here, we keep all the things he likes to eat. He works so hard to protect the land here, he likes to get his own back, you see. But I will look after you … to a point.'

Jack started to pay more attention to the old woman, and he started to feel really quite nervous. What did she mean, 'to a point'?

She led Jack along a large branch, into a rocky hillside, and into another long tunnel of winding stone stairs, until they came to a large kitchen with a good fire burning in the grate. Everything was twice the normal size, and Jack had to perch on the edge of a chair and let the old woman bring him food.

It wasn't long before Jack found himself tucking into bread and cheese and pickle, and gulping down great flagons of water and even a pint of cider. He was just starting to forget his fears and enjoy himself, when a slow drum beat started to thud outside, getting louder: 'Boom … *Boom* … BOOM.'

'That's my son. Quick! In here!' and the woman opened a cupboard door, as there was a great CRASH and the whole kitchen shook.

Jack had no choice but to crawl into the cupboard. Even a giant's cupboard was ever so slightly too small for him, but he managed to curl up tightly and pull the door to.

Not a moment too soon. Jack could hear the giant crashing into the kitchen, shouting 'MOTHER!'

And we all know what the giant said next:

Fi, Fi, Fo, Fum!
I smell the blood of an Englishman.
Be he alive or be he dead
I'll grind his bones to make my bread.

This didn't faze the old woman in the slightest. 'Oh, my dear, it's nothing but the children in the trees. The wind changed today,' she said.

The giant growled, but he appeared to be satisfied, and Jack had to stay in the cupboard, all cramped and keeping as quiet as possible, trying not to breathe, while the giant's mother prepared a meal for her son. How was he going to get out of this one?

Jack peeked through a crack in the cupboard door, and he noticed two things. The first was the giant. There was a real giant! He was twice as big as a human, with very pointed teeth, and he was very hairy … but his hair was green. His beard curled around his chin like old moss and lichen, and the hair on his body made him look as if he'd been left outside all winter.

The second thing was that Jack could smell roasted meat, and he wondered whether this was the stench of roasted human flesh, and the crackling of human skin over the fire. It could be him next! Through the crack in the cupboard door, he watched the giant devour his supper, crunching the bones, picking out the sinews from between his teeth. The bile rose in Jack's throat, and he tried everything he could not to be sick.

The meal went on and on. After several hours had gone by, the giant at last finished his supper, and said, 'MOTHER! Bring me my gold and silver.' The old woman, with difficulty, dragged four huge sacks into the kitchen and left him before he could hit her; and the giant started counting out piles of gold and silver coin on to the kitchen table, stacking them in heaps and making pretty patterns.

'One, two, three …

'Fifteen, sixteen, seventeen …

'Sixty-five, sixty-six … they'll never get hold of this, now, will they?'

'One hundred and twenty, one hundred and twenty-one … Yes, that'll learn them.'

'Four hundred and eighty-one …'

Then eventually the giant heaped the coins back into the bags, and his head lolled, and he nodded off in the chair.

Jack waited until he thought the giant was fully asleep, and then with great care he opened the cupboard and crept across the kitchen, his arms and legs barely working from cramp.

Jack reached up to the table and took two heavy handfuls of coins, put them in his pyjama pockets, and ran for his life, out of the kitchen, down the stairs, along the branch, through the tree, out of the little door and into the woods, praying that he could remember the right direction to go. He made his way as best he could, all through the night by the moonlight, and as the sun came up, there was the top of the beanstalk poking through the floor of the woods, with the rag tied to it. Jack climbed down, with some difficulty, trying not to lose the gold as he went.

His mother was delighted to see Jack safe and sound, and even more delighted to see the gold and silver. They had the cottage repaired and well furnished, she got some help with the garden, and they lived comfortably. They ate an awful lot of beans all through the seasons from the beanstalk, as it never seemed to stop producing them.

❦

Time went by, and Jack thought a lot about the giant, and the giant's treasure, and he found himself wanting more adventures. You know what it's like when the memory is better than the actual event? Well, that's how it was with Jack.

This time he decided to wear a disguise. He combed his hair differently and tried to grow what he could of a beard. 'It's a plan,' thought Jack. 'She won't recognise me.'

Early one morning, Jack climbed the beanstalk, armed this time with food and water. What a climb! He was sure this time that the beanstalk was higher than before. It felt as if he was about half way up, and Jack looked back to the land, rich with wheat just starting to turn golden. But it wasn't just wheat. There were traces in the land where hedges used to be, and where houses used to be; curves and stripes across the landscape from many generations ago. And for the first time Jack wondered about the history of the place where he had grown up, and who had lived there before him.

By the time Jack reached the top, he had used all his supplies and he was ravenous; and there he was, in the same land again.

But was it the same land? There were no trees to be seen, apart from a few scrappy willows. Instead there were tall reeds everywhere, taller than his head; graceful swallowtail butterflies; the occasional plop of a water vole into the water below; and the air was alive, buzzing insects everywhere, mosquitoes landing on him for a tasty meal. There in front of him, almost leading from the beanstalk, was an old track made of tree trunks that someone had lain over the water, through the reeds and the mud to make it passable.

He made sure that the rag was still tied to the beanstalk, and followed the sun until the sunset, swatting mosquitoes for the whole time, and with midges caught in his straggly beard and his hair, crawling and itching and biting. There was only a track in the boggiest places, and Jack found that he had to squelch his way along through dark mud and water. It wasn't a pleasant journey. At last he came to the clearing and the huge tree. There was the little door at its base, and there was the old woman.

'Please,' said Jack, 'do you have food and water?'

'Well,' said the woman, 'I could invite you in – but a while back I did the same and the lad stole treasure from my son, and since then he has been very suspicious. He guards what's important to him, and he loves to eat human flesh when he can get it. For good reason, given the way that most of you behave. Or perhaps you're different …?'

The old woman was looking at Jack a little too closely for his liking, but she let him in and led him to the kitchen as before. Jack feasted on bread and cheese, but it wasn't long before the ground shook and the giant arrived. 'Quick,' she said, and she hid Jack in an old wood store at the end of the kitchen. Jack watched through a crack in the door as the giant strode into the kitchen. 'MOTHER! I smell human flesh!'

'No, dear, it's just the children hanging in the larder,' said the giant's mother casually; and she prepared and cooked her son's supper in front of Jack's eyes. The giant was a very slow eater, smacking his chops and making sure he got every last scrap of meat off the bones.

It did end, after several hours. The giant then roared, 'MOTHER! Bring me my hen.' Sure enough, the giant's mother brought in an ordinary looking, normal-sized brown hen and sat it down on the huge kitchen table.

'LAY!' said the giant.

The hen looked a little surprised, and squawked slightly, and the giant picked it up and there on the table was an egg. Then Jack saw the glint of gold … this egg was made of pure gold! The giant grinned all across his huge green mossy face, took the gold egg, put it in a basket on the floor, and put the hen back down on the table. 'LAY!'

And so it went on, for what seemed like forever. The giant's mother went to bed and still the giant was roaring, 'LAY!' But eventually, the giant started to get dozy, and sitting in his kitchen chair, his head lolled and he was fast asleep. The snores shook the kitchen, the table and the hen, which was looking a bit stressed by this point.

Jack waited for a sensible amount of time – and as much more time as he could stand in the wood store – and then slowly, very slowly, opened the door and crept out into the kitchen. Then he seized the hen and ran out of that kitchen and out of the tree and across the clearing and down the long, squelchy wooden track towards the beanstalk.

Well, the hen was lighter than the gold and silver, although it did fidget inside his shirt and made climbing down the beanstalk a little awkward at times. Jack found his mother weeping in the little house, and she was overjoyed to see him; and he said, 'Mother! There's some magic to show you!' He put the hen down on the kitchen table.

'It's a hen. Hens aren't magic,' said his mother, and she sighed. 'Oh, Jack, you are a fool.'

'Wait,' said Jack. 'This one's different. LAY!'

The hen let out a small squawk and its eyes watered.

Jack picked up the hen, and there was an egg made of pure gold.

The hen made Jack and his mother very rich, and they could buy all the food and clothing they wanted, although they stayed in the little house, and they never needed to buy any beans, that was for sure.

~

Jack couldn't forget the beanstalk, which was still there in the garden, still green as ever, still producing beans for them. It became an obsession; and early one morning at harvest-time, he decided to make another journey. He had prepared this time, with all kind of fancy climbing kit, gadgets, and dehydrated food for convenience; and yet he still climbed the beanstalk with some difficulty, finding that ropes and pins only complicate matters when you're trying to climb a giant plant.

About halfway up, Jack stopped and looked back at his homeland. This time, he noticed how little green there was in the land of golden wheat, how few wild things were allowed to grow and be glad, how isolated and tiny their little patch of land was. The beanstalk he was climbing was the wildest thing there, by far, and the place he was going to was much more interesting; and yet he felt a pang for home, looking down on it.

He found the land at the top of the beanstalk; at least, he thought it was the same land. This time there were meadows stretching as far as he could see, smothered in oxeye daisy and purple vetch and knapweed and yellow trefoil and bedstraw, and clouds of blue butterflies as he walked. Occasionally he saw a herd of ponies in the distance, but they didn't come near; occasionally he wandered through boggy woodland full of ancient alder and willow trees; and he travelled towards the setting sun.

Finally Jack arrived at the giant's tree. There was the old woman again, and at first she wouldn't let him in. 'You take

too much, you little people, and give no thanks in return!'
she said. But Jack won her round eventually, and she grum-
bled her way up the stairs, saying 'Well, perhaps there is
more for him to learn; on his head be it!'

Jack had a fine meal, and when the giant arrived the old
woman hid Jack in the kitchen copper. The giant roared,
'MOTHER! I smell fresh meat!' and this time, no matter
what his mother did to dissuade him, he started hunting
all over the kitchen. He was getting closer to Jack. He
approached the copper, but never lifted the lid; and so, tired
of searching, he then crunched his way through another
human meal, which Jack could only listen to this time, and
he was quite glad not to be able to see.

Jack heard the giant roar, 'MOTHER! Bring me my
harp.' Then he heard the giant roar 'PLAY!' and the most
beautiful music started. Jack heard the old woman's voice
say, 'I'll just go to bed then, dear, shall I?' Then the harp
continued to play so sweetly that even Jack was nearly
lulled to sleep. He waited until the giant started snoring
loud enough to make the kitchen copper ring with the
noise. It was time to move.

But Jack couldn't get out of the copper. He had to rock
backwards and forwards until eventually the copper rolled
on to its side with an enormous CLANK. Jack froze,
waiting to see if the giant had woken up with the noise. But
he didn't. Jack got out of the copper as quietly as he could,
crept over to where the giant was sleeping, and reached up
to the table.

As soon as Jack touched the harp it called out loudly,
'Master! MASTER!'

The giant's eyes snapped open and his brow furrowed as
he looked at Jack; he started to his feet, but he was so drunk
that he could hardly stand. Poor Jack ran as fast as he could;

if the giant had been sober, he would have overtaken Jack in no time, but as it was, Jack was halfway down the beanstalk before the giant reached the top. The giant was roaring all kinds of obscenities but the only words Jack could understand were: 'You take too much! You take too much!'

The beanstalk was shaking all the way down as the giant crashed through above Jack; but as soon as Jack touched the ground, he ran to the woodshed for an axe, and started hacking at the base of the great stalks. One, two, three stems he cut, and still the beanstalk remained and the giant was getting closer. Four, five, six stems and the great ladder to the sky started to collapse, and the giant with it. He crashed to the ground among the golden wheat in the field next to Jack's house, and then there was silence.

Jack ran over to where the giant had fallen and cracked his neck. As he stared at the body, it changed in front of his eyes. The head and body started to dissolve and sink down into the soil. In its place, plants of all kinds began to germinate and grow and curl their green way round the giant's shape, grasses and bindweeds and nettles and goosegrass and meadowsweet and honeysuckle. The plants grew outwards across the wheat fields and reclaimed them, along ditches, right along the valley, and they transformed the place back into wild wood and tangle and reedbed and patches of wild meadow.

And from that time to the present day, that particular part of England, the dark soil and the hard-worked land, has been full of the green energy of the spring and summer and plants growing up towards the sun. No matter how much people have tried to tame it with machines and chemicals, they have failed. It's a place where nature has taken the land back, and the wild means to stay; and the humans have learned that they have to share.

Jack's mother was delighted to see her son, and Jack promised to her that he would look after her and be more considerate in the future. And they are both living there in great happiness still, with Jack's wife and all the family around them, and all the wild plants and animals outside, and they grow all their own food. I know, because I visited them only last week.

And I can tell you that the cottage still carries the very English whiff of slightly overcooked runner beans.

THE HORNBEAM TREE

Hornbeam is a curious, tough and resilient tree. Its trunk is elliptical in section and the leaves look something like beech, although hornbeam is more closely related to the hazel. In the old days it was called 'ironwood' because of the hardness of the timber, and 'lanthorn' because it burned with such a bright flame. Hornbeam is a native of south and east England.

This rather satisfying story reminds me of the time I discovered a grisly row of small mammal bodies that had been strung up in the woods by a gamekeeper in Norfolk. It seems that animals need the help of the tough old hornbeam tree to get their revenge.

There was a brutal man, who loved to hunt for nothing more than the joy of killing things. He would kill any animal, no matter how small, and if it was large he would enjoy torturing the animal before putting it out of its misery. He would hang the bodies of the animals on fences and tree branches to frighten anyone who passed by, animal or human alike.

The hunter wasn't the most popular man, as you might imagine, and all the animals were afraid of being killed and strung up by him. His favourite tree for hanging his dead quarry was a big hornbeam, with branches that spread out in all directions, some so long that they touched the ground.

The Hart Royal of the woodland grew angry. 'Humans don't dare to stop this hunter in case he causes problems for them. But all the animals of our greenwood suffer. All of us have been hunted or affected by him, all of us. We have to do something to stop him.'

'Not now,' said his hind. 'I'll have my calf any time now. I can only move slowly.'

'I don't need you to run fast. I am quick enough for us both. I just need your royal courage, and that I know you have. Of course, there is always a risk that he may kill us both.'

'He has killed too many of us,' said the hind. 'So we must take the risk. What do you want me to do?'

'Go and stand under the big hornbeam tree, close to its trunk. The boughs are higher there and then they sweep right down to the ground among the bracken and the brambles. Stay close to the trunk of the tree, and don't be afraid. I will hide in the bracken and lie on top of the low branches on the ground. We must snare the hunter ourselves or die trying.'

So the hind, with the warm sunlight shimmering on her chestnut-red flanks, walked slowly to stand close to the tree trunk and tried not to think of the safety of her coming calf. She stood still and quite proud. The stag hid as he had said.

Presently the hunter came creeping up to the tree and he saw the outline of the hind against the smooth grey bark of the hornbeam tree. He drew his short sword and moved towards her slowly, and she pretended not to see him. A hind in calf, hemmed in by the branches of the tree; she would be easy prey for the hunter. He had only to creep a short distance to reach her.

He bent low and started to crawl towards the hind.

Then the Hart Royal took his weight and his hooves off the end of a great hornbeam bough, which sprang up and back with the hunter himself dangling from it, high in the air and shouting. And there he stayed – I will leave you to decide just how long he was hanging from the hornbeam tree.

The hind moved to a safer space away from the hornbeam, and the Hart Royal joined her. 'Now we'll find a safe place for our coming youngster,' he said. 'You're the bravest mother in the greenwood.'

6

Ripening Time

Where there's bracken there's gold,
Where there's gorse there's silver,
Where there's heather there's poverty.

Cumbria

By the beginning of August, the first fruits are beginning to ripen and the harvest begins. Apart from the Lammas flush of the oak leaves and the regrowth of grass after the hay cut, most plants and trees across Britain and Ireland are starting to look a little bit scruffy, a little bit sleepy. The year has properly turned, and although we won't let the summer go yet, the dew in the mornings is that little bit heavier.

THAT'S ENOUGH TO GO ON WITH

Wild strawberries are an absolute delight if you can find them. William Morris thought the same; he a thrush swoop down to take a wild strawberry and was inspired to create his 'Strawberry Thief' pattern. It is difficult to stop eating strawberries of any kind, though, and here is a cautionary tale.

There was a little boy and a little girl, whose mother and father were dead. They lived with their granny in a little hut, in the little hamlet next to the haunted wood, the place called the Little Men's Wood, that nobody dared to venture into.

Now the little boy and the little girl and the granny never had enough to eat between them. All they had was a nanny goat, who produced a small amount of milk that they had to share. But the granny taught the children well, and she always said, 'Good manners will take you a long way.' The people in the little hamlet liked them for it. Sometimes they would give the children a bit of food here and there – some cabbage leaves, a turnip, a few bones for soup, the ends of the bread, even a little bit of scrumpy – and if they were offered still more, the children always said, 'No more. That's enough to go on with. Thank you kindly,' and so everyone was appreciated in the proper manner.

All the land around the hamlet was owned by a rich farmer who lived in a grand farmhouse close by. He seemed to have everything: orchards, and a fine herd of cows, and corn ricks, and barns, and vegetable fields. But he sold every last cabbage leaf, he counted all his turnips, and he fed all his crusts to his pigs; he never had any meat of his own, because it cost money, and so he grew richer, and richer, and richer.

When the little boy and the little girl took their goat to find grass, they had to go by the side of the farmer's fields, and his dog chased them away and bared his teeth. And the farmer's fat children used to go to the poor little hut and throw stones at the old granny picking up twigs. They taunted her, and told horrid rhymes, and said she was a witch and stole the milk from his cows. Well, that was a lie. But the little boy and the little girl and the goat had to walk much further away to find grass that wasn't owned by the farmer.

One day the poor hungry goat strained and broke its tether, and ran from the lane right into the Little Men's Wood, where the grass grew thick. The little boy and the little girl called out and ran up to the edge of the woods, but then they stopped.

'We can't go in here! The little men will get us!'

'But we have to fetch the nanny goat, we can't lose her.'

So the little boy called out, 'Please forgive our hungry goat – may we come into the woods to get her?'

There was silence from the woods.

'Er … thank you … kindly,' called out the little girl.

And into the woods they crept, with twigs crunching underfoot and great branches looming over their heads. They didn't have to go far before they came to a grassy clearing, and there was the nanny goat, eating and eating for all she was worth.

But the little goat wasn't eating grass, she was eating strawberries. The floor of the clearing was thick with tiny bright red strawberries, plump and inviting. The floor was almost scarlet, there were so many.

'Do you think we're allowed any?' said the little girl.

The boy stepped forward and talked to the thin air. 'We are very hungry, and so is our granny at home. May we pick a handful of strawberries?'

This time there was a low chuckle, and a voice: the kind of voice that creates mischief. 'Of course,' it said. 'Pick all the strawberries you want.'

So, while the goat carried on eating, the boy and the girl picked a double handful of the berries each, and they only tried a few. They were good strawberries! They wanted to eat more and more. In fact, the more strawberries they ate, the more they craved. It was a hunger and a craving for food they had never felt before. It was a magical craving. It was a spell.

But then they remembered their manners, and the manners won over the cravings. The girl said to the thin air, 'No more, please – that's enough to go on with, and thank you kindly.'

As soon as they said thank you, their craving for more strawberries stopped. As soon as they said thank you, the magic was overridden and the spell was broken. Even the goat was able to stop gobbling strawberries and go with them safe out of the wood, without a complaint.

When they got back to the little hut, the granny was delighted, and of course she said thank you after the strawberries were finished: but she had an idea. They saved a few strawberries and planted them in the garden to see what would happen. In no time at all, the tendrils and leaves of wild strawberry plants were running across the little plot of land, and new fruits were appearing on the plants. The new fruits kept on forming, no matter what the season, and no matter how many they picked and ate. All the boy and the girl and the granny had to do was to remember to say thank you after they had eaten enough, which was no trouble to them at all.

After that, they never went short of rich milk, and they never went hungry again.

One day the rich farmer drove by the little hut. It was a cold day and there was a smattering of snow on the ground:

but he could see the red strawberries peeping out of the leaves and the snow. He got out of his carriage and went into the hut, without even knocking at the door.

'Those are my strawberries, that I grow to sell! Where did you steal them from?' he shouted. Well, that was a lie.

The boy and the girl and the granny told him that they had come from the Little Men's Wood.

'That wood is mine too!' he yelled. Well, that was true, but only as far as the Land Registry cared.

Then the farmer went out to their little patch of land without leave, and picked every strawberry he could see, and began to eat them. 'Mmmm! These are good!' The children and their granny watched him and said nothing. They knew that when he had gone, another crop would ripen again in time for supper.

When the farmer had finished every ripe strawberry there, he wanted more. 'Where did you find them?' They gave him directions, and off he rushed in his grand carriage as fast as he could. He barged into the wood with his great big feet and found the clearing. There were hundreds and hundreds of bright red strawberries, growing in the snow.

The farmer ate, and he ate, and he didn't ask leave. He ate, and he ate, and he couldn't stop to say 'please'. He ate, and he ate, and he didn't know how to say 'That's enough', or 'Thank you kindly'. He ate and he ate all day, and all night, and all the week through.

When Sunday came, and still he was eating, he burst with a bang, and where the farmer used to be, there was a horrible, red, sticky mess.

THE LAST OF THE PICTS

Since ancient times, ale has been made in Scotland using heather tops and sometimes bog-myrtle leaves, making a sweet, dry, potent brew. Those who drank a lot of it were said to acquire a speckled face, like a salmon. Excavations of Neolithic remains on the isle of Rhum have found traces of a fermented drink made using heather flowers.

Robert Louis Stevenson was so taken with the story of heather ale that he wrote a poem about it:

> From the bonny bells of heather
> They brewed a drink long-syne,
> Was sweeter far then honey,
> Was stronger far than wine …

There is another tale of a Highland clan warming heather ale over the fire on a cold winter night. The steam from the hot ale cooled against the stone roof and dripped into a drinking-cup, and this is how Uisge-beatha, *the 'Water of Life', or whisky, was discovered.*

This version of the story comes from Shetland.

The first people ever to live on Shetland were called the Picts. Short wee people they were, with arms longer than they should have been. They had so much red curly hair on their heads that when it rained – which was very often – they could use it to keep themselves dry.

The Picts brewed a magic drink (*leann fraoch*) from the purple heather flowers. It was somewhere between a beer and a spirit, and everyone who tried it wanted more, but the secret of how to make it was guarded well. There was

plenty of heather on the land, and plenty of Picts brewing it up, and the special ale flowed freely on the happy islands of Shetland. The recipe was handed down from father to son, along with strict instructions never to tell a soul. As the years went on, and battles were fought and land became more precious, still the Picts never lost the secret of the heather ale.

One year the Norsemen surprised the islanders with their invasion and killed most of them, apart from one man and his teenage son. The only reason these two were spared? The Norsemen wanted to know how to make the famous heather ale, and here was their chance to learn the secret.

Trussed up and held captive, neither father nor son would speak. The Norse king ordered, and he implored, and he begged, but they would give up no words. The sea-king tried torture; he stretched the man's arms from his body, and set fire to his toes, and made him yell with pain. The father then said, 'Kill the lad, and then I'll tell you.'

What? The Picts were meant to be honourable people: how could he want his son killed? But the Norse king wanted the secret. He ordered that the boy be killed in front of his father.

The father's eyes glazed over, like ice. When his son had gurgled his last breath, he said: 'Now, you can kill me slow, or you can kill me fast, it doesn't matter. You shall never learn the secrets of our race from me, and I am the last of the Picts. My son was a weak youth, and might have told; but you can never force me.'

The king of the Norsemen was startled at this, and he realised that the biggest punishment for this man would be allowing him to live. So the last of the Picts was thrown into prison, and lived for years and decades with no company, never tasting his beloved heather ale again. Despite torture every so often, when the king got a thirst for the ale, he never passed on the recipe. After many empty, lonely years he died a bedridden, blind old man, and the secret of heather ale died with him.

And after that there were no more Picts in Shetland.

TOM FITZPATRICK AND THE LEPRECHAUN

Ragwort gets a bad press because it is poisonous to stock. Farmers have a duty to control ragwort under the Dangerous Weeds Act, and ragwort pulling is a horrible task. But it is a beautiful plant, food-plant to the dramatic orange and black striped caterpillars of the cinnabar moth. This story comes from Kildare.

Tom Fitzpatrick was the eldest son of a rich farmer, and they lived close to the river Liffey. Tom was in no hurry with life. When this story happened, he had just turned twenty-nine, and was as clever and good-looking a boy as any in the whole county of Kildare.

One fine day at harvest-time, Tom didn't feel like working, and he was rambling by himself along the sunny side of a hedge. He heard a clacking noise just a little way in front of him, from within the hedge. It sounded like a stonechat, but surely it was late in the season for them?

So Tom crept on, quiet as he could, to get sight of whatever was making the noise. And as usually happens, the noise stopped.

Then Tom spied through the leaves of the hedge, and what did he see on the ground in the middle but a big brown pitcher, and next to it was a scrawny little old man, sporting a leather apron and a battered old brown hat, and he was fetching a little wooden stool, and he scrambled on to it, dipped his flask down into the pitcher, and sat down to drink.

'Well, I never!' said Tom to himself. 'I often heard tell of the leprechauns, but never believed in them. Let me think now. If I leave him alone and lose my luck, I'll be mad. They say you should never take your eyes off them, or they'll escape.'

Tom now crept round slowly, with his eyes fixed on the little man just as a cat does with a mouse. When he got quite close, he called out, 'Morning to yer, honest man.'

The little man lifted up his head and fixed Tom with a beady little gaze. 'And to you.' It was a sharp little voice.

'What've you got in the pitcher there?' said Tom.

'It's good beer.'

'Thunder and fire, man, where did you get that?'

'Get it? Well, I made it; out of heather tops.'

'I can't be believing that. You'll be needing malt for beer.'

'I'm telling the real truth,' said the leprechaun, 'did you never hear tell of the Picts?'

'To be sure I did,' said Tom. 'They used to live here, but they all died.'

The leprechaun coughed. 'Hem, is that all you know on the matter? The Picts were from the little people, and they taught their kin to make beer out of the heath, and the secret's been with my family ever since.'

'Is it time to share that secret, and let me try it?' said Tom.

'I'll tell you, young man, it'd be better for you to look after your father's farm, than to be bothering decent folk with your idiot questions. While you're idling away there, the cows have broken into the oats back home.'

Well, no lazy man likes to have his faults pointed out too sharply, for fear he might have to do some work. Tom went red in the face, and he was just about to turn around, when he remembered he shouldn't take his eyes from the leprechaun. He thrust his hand into the hedgerow, grabbed the leprechaun, and at the same time he upset the pitcher, and all the beer drained into the roots of the hedge.

So Tom never did try the heather beer, and he swore loudly. 'Because of that ... I think you should be telling me where I can find some fairy treasure.' Tom's glare was so wicked, and his grip so tight, that the little man was quite scared.

'Of course,' said the leprechaun, gasping for breath. 'I'll show you a place a little way from here, where there's a crock of gold been buried these past ages. Over that way.'

Tom held the leprechaun fast in his hand, and never took his eyes off him, and they started walking the way the leprechaun said, right through the middle of hedges and over

ditches, and through a deep sodden bog; the most difficult path that Tom had ever travelled.

At last they came to a wide field full of yellow ragweed (*bolyawn buies*). The leprechaun pointed to a big bolyawn. 'That's it, there. Dig under that plant, and you'll find a crock full 'golden of guineas'.

Tom had no spade, so he decided to run home and fetch one. So that he could tell the plant from all the others, he took his black and orange handkerchief and tied it round the yellow flowerheads of the plant, with care to still keep the little man in his gaze.

'I suppose,' said the leprechaun casually, 'you've no further need for me now?'

'No, you can go away,' said Tom, with bad grace; all he could think about was the gold.

'Goodbye, Tom Fitzpatrick,' said the leprechaun, 'much good may you do with what you'll get.' And he disappeared.

So Tom ran as fast as he could back to the farm, got a spade, and ran fast back to the field of bolyawns; but when he got back, every single bolyawn in the field had a black and orange hanky twisted around its yellow flowerheads, the same as his own. There was no way Tom was going to go digging up ten good Irish acres of land, with yellow flowers and black and orange hankies as far as the eye could see.

So Tom flung the spade on his shoulder and dawdled home dejected; and what did he get from the leprechaun in the end? A rare talent. He became famous for his creative cursing, because that happened every time he thought of the leprechaun.

THE FINE FIELD OF FLAX

This beautiful Orkney story is about lint, or flax, which has been cultivated for its linen fibres and linseed oil across Britain for thousands of years. Its blue flowers persist in the wild, near to where it has been grown. The tale carries more than the joy of wild foraging; in this instance the plant is a life-changer, and a binder of community between estranged people. Blaeberries, or bilberries, were used in ancient times as a purple dye.

The Gloup of Root is a place on the east shore of South Ronaldsay, near Halcro Head. It's a great chasm some way from the cliff edge, connected with the sea by a long cave. The ground at the seaward side of the Gloup of Root is untilled, but it carries signs and marks of ancient cultivation.

Many, many years ago, on the island of South Ronaldsay, there was a lass who gave birth to a child when she was scarcely more than a child herself. The bairn was a lass too, as bonnie and winsome as her mother.

The new mother was young and she was innocent. Her mother and father asked her about how the child had come to be, she said that she did not know and could not tell. When she was asked who the father of the baby was, she said that she truly had no notion and had never met anyone who it could be. They tried to get her talking and to tell more of her predicament, but the lass said calmly and firmly that there was nothing more to say – and that was that.

Her folk were keen to be forgiving of the lass, but the kirk and the kirk's people were watching, and they were judging, and they would not let them be. Ministers and elders and high-up people, all of them men, interrogated the girl again and again about the father, but she could say no more than she had told her parents. And they would not believe her. Nobody in the town believed her. People passed the family in silence with cold, hard stares and accusation written on their faces. They judged the lass by their own narrow stand-ards, and they found her wanting: they could not understand her innocence.

That poor lass and her child were treated badly from that point on. Everybody in the little community seemed to be against them and made their lives as difficult as they could. As the years went by, they had to struggle just for food and clothes, and nobody gave them work or charity. They were not allowed to sow their grain, or grow their lint in the common fields like other people did. They lived on the edges. And day in, day out, they had to suffer the taunts and the calls: 'Slut! Whore! Get away from here.' The whole town acted as if it were a duty for them to be cruel, and the lass and her child were turned into outcasts. Often, they walked the seashore for what they could find or forage.

In time, the bonnie little child became a handsome young lass, and then a fine young woman. Her mother was sad that her girl had to wear rags – for that was all they could afford.

One day in late summer, the bonnie lassie was wandering by the sea, by the place they call the Gloup of Root, when she came across a fine field of lint growing between the gloup and the sea. It was far better and stronger lint than any that grew in South Ronaldsay, and it was ready to harvest. She went back to tell her mother; and they both uprooted and carried away armfuls of this lint, which seemed to belong to nobody.

The mother treated the lint, first by removing the seed heads, retting (rotting) the stems in water, drying and then scutching (bruising) and hackling (separating) the stems to remove the flax fibres. The fibres were spun and the fabric woven. Eventually it was soft linen cloth, fit for a queen.

Then she made the linen into a fine, full-skirted dress for her daughter. Finally, the dress was dyed with blaeberries from the moor: a rich, clear purple. Mother and daughter agreed that they had never seen such a fine dress.

The lassie was wearing the purple dress when the laird came past a few days later. He could not take his eyes off her, and he must have told his son all about her; for the young man came to find her, and fell in love with her, and married her. After that, the name-calling and the judgement didn't matter so much any more.

> And it's all because of the fields, two, three,
> Where the flax grew so strong
> Between the chasm and the sea.

I bore him two sons
They travelled afar,
Yet they never forgot
The fields, two, three,
Where the flax grew so strong
Between the chasm and the sea.

THE CURSE OF PANTANNAS

Wildflower grassland, the old permanent pasture or greensward, used to cover the fields of Britain, usually managed through hay cutting and grazing. Managed the old-fashioned way, it can contain 'fairy rings', caused by mushrooms, and also a riotous mixture of wild grasses, herbs and flowers. Sadly, many of these wild plants are now rarities, with a staggering ninety-seven percent of our wildflower meadows lost in the last seventy-five years. More are being ploughed up all the time.

Why has this happened? Well, modern farming rarely makes space for nature. Permanent pasture is ploughed up for arable crops or intensive grassland, all monocultures of plants specially bred to push food production to the maximum. I've spent much of my working life trying to persuade farmers and politicians to value the little wildflower grassland we have left.

This story, from Glamorgan, tells of a farmer who ploughs up his greensward to get rid of the fairy rings and destroy the joy in the land. It's a story about responsibility, and how the effects of land mismanagement echo through the generations, with everyone left the poorer for it.

In the county of Glamorgan, near to Merthyr Tydfil, there is a hollow in the land that some call Pant yr Aros, 'Hollow of the Staying', and others call Pant yr Hanes, 'Hollow of the Legend'. Centuries ago there was a farm in this place called Pantannas.

Centuries before that, a particularly ill-tempered farmer lived at the farm at Pantannas. This farmer complained about the fairies, the Fair Folk, who in those days could still be seen dancing in the fairy rings on the fields to the light of the moon, bringing gladness and music to the land, in among the cowslips, the orchids in the springtime and the purple knapweed and the orange-yellow bird's foot trefoil in the summer. The fairies sang songs of the flowers, the butterflies and the birds that shared the fields with them, about the glory of nature, and about the joy of simply living there.

'What have they got so be so happy about?' growled the farmer. 'They keep me awake with their singing. I'd be happier if I were rid of them for good.' Not being able to think of any fairy-clearing methods of his own, he went to an old wise woman in the village and told her that he wanted rid of the fairies on his farm.

'Are you sure you want to do this?' said the wise woman. 'The fairies are of another world, and they don't take kindly to human authority.'

'Authority? This is my land,' said the farmer, 'and I'll do what I want with it!'

'Very well,' said the wise woman. 'If you are determined, then you must promise me a day and a night of milking on your farm, and I will tell you.'

'Done! An easy bargain,' said the farmer.

'Wherever you see a fairy ring in your fields, plough the fairy ring backwards and forth with an iron plough, then plough the whole field, and sow it with wheat,' she said. 'When the fairies find the greensward and the wild flowers gone, they won't come back.'

The farmer took her advice. He yoked his oxen and drove his iron ploughshare twice through every circle in which the fairies had danced at night, cursing the fairies as he went. Then he ploughed the fields over, and sowed them with wheat.

Just as the wise woman had said, the nightly sounds of dance and song ceased, and no fairy was seen in the fields of Pantannas from that day onwards. There was instead a clean and tidy silence across the whole farm, and in time the farmer's grumbling turned into whistling, and he stood a little taller, thinking great things about himself.

One evening that year in the late spring, when the wheat in the fields was green and growing, the farmer was walking home in the pink haze of the sunset, when a tiny little man in a red coat appeared, unsheathed a little sword, and pointed the sword straight at the farmer, saying:

Dial a ddaw, y mae gerllaw.
Vengeance comes, fast it approaches.

After saying this, the little man disappeared. Had the farmer imagined it? He tried to laugh; but there was something about the pointed anger of the little man which made him feel very uncomfortable.

Spring turned into summer, and summer into autumn, and nothing happened. The farmer began to think that the little man in the red coat had only been a dream.

In the harvest-time of that year, when the corn was golden in the fields and ripe for the sickle, the farmer and his family were going to bed one night, when they heard a mighty noise outside, loud enough to shake the stone farmhouse. They all heard a loud voice, coming as if from the ground itself, and it said:

Daw dial.
Vengeance comes.

Next morning, as the farmer walked his land, he found no ear of golden corn, no straw remaining. All his crop of wheat had been burned to black ashes by the fairies.

As he walked, almost beside himself with horror and grief, the farmer was met by the same little man as before, who pointed his sword at the farmer in anger and said:

Nid yw ond dechreu.
It only begins.

The farmer's face turned as white as milk, and he began to gibber. 'I'm sorry! I didn't mean harm! I have made a mistake. Look – why don't you come back to my fields? You can dance, and sing, and I will let the meadow grow again, and I promise not to interfere again, I promise.'

The red-coated little man looked stern, and his sword didn't move. 'No, the word of the king has gone out: he will have his revenge on you, and no power can stop it.'

At this, the farmer promptly burst into tears, and his sobbing and pleading was so heartfelt that the little man at last took some pity on him. 'If you truly repent, then I can only ask. I will come again at sunset in three days' time, and I will tell you my lord's decision.'

When the time came on the third day, the little man was waiting for the farmer at the same spot in the fields. 'The king's word,' he said, 'cannot be recalled, and vengeance must come. Still, since you are truly sorry and keen to set the damage right, the curse shall not fall in your time, nor that of your children, but it will await your distant descendants.'

This promise comforted the farmer. He let the cropped fields turn to fallow, and gradually over the next years, the grasses and the wild flowers returned. The farmer watched and waited anxiously. In time, the dark green fairy rings of grass grew again, the fairies danced by the light of the moon, and the sounds of music and singing gladdened the fields as of old.

There were reminders. The dread voice came back at times, repeating the threat:

Daw dial.
Vengeance will come.

But when the family heard the voice again, they were so accustomed to it that they believed nothing would come of the threat. The years went by, the farmer passed away in peaceful old age, and his children followed him to the churchyard without feeling any effects of the curse from the king of the fairies.

⁂

More than a century after the farmer's mistake, his great-great grandson, Madoc, was the sole heir of Pantannas. Madoc was betrothed to beautiful Teleri, the daughter of the squire of Pen Craig Daf, a nearby farm. When the wedding was only a few weeks away, near to Christmas-time, Madoc's family threw a lavish party at Pantannas farmhouse to celebrate their son's betrothal. Teleri and all her family were invited.

It was a merry celebration, with fine food and ale flowing. Everyone from the two families was there, seated around the hearth, sharing tales and stories. Teleri's father was mid-song when he was interrupted by a loud voice, not from their own company. It was a rich, deep voice, and sounded almost as if it were coming from the river outside. It said:

Daeth amser ymddial.
The time for revenge is come.

A silence fell on the gathering. They rushed outside to see if they could find some source for the voice, if it would come again: but they couldn't make out another sound apart from the angry noise of the river Taff rushing past the house. Puzzled, the families went back into the house. They gradually chased away their fears with ale and song, and continued the party.

Again, above the sounds of mirth and the noise of the river as it boiled over the boulders, there was a clear, deep voice:

Daeth yr amser.
The time is come.

A dread noise crashed around them, and the house shook violently to its foundations. The whole company were speechless with fear. Into the silence, a filthy hooded hag appeared at the farmhouse window and leered at them. Teleri's brother, bolder than the rest, called out, 'What do you want with us, ugly thing?'

'I'll have nothing to do with you, chatterer,' said the hag. 'I had come to tell of the doom awaiting this house, and the other that hopes to be allied with it, but as you have insulted me, the veil which conceals it shall not be lifted by me. I will only tell you this: a maiden's heart is like a ship on the coast, unable to reach the harbour because the captain has been lost.' With that, the hag vanished.

When she had gone, the deep voice from the river Taff started again, more loudly than before, and repeating over and over in a relentless chant:

Daeth amser ymddial.
The time for vengeance has come.

Terror and gloom fell on the house then. The guests all left
for home as quickly as they could. Madoc took Teleri back
to Pen Craig Daf, saying all that he could to dispel her fears,
for she was terrified at the prophecy of the hag and paralysed
with fright at its meaning.

All through the long hours of darkness, Madoc's parents
waited for him to return to Pantannas after taking Teleri home.
But by morning, their son had still not returned. His father
and mother, already shaken by the vision of the hag and the
strange voices which had interrupted their feast, were beside
themselves with anxiety for the safety of their only child. As
the day wore on, without any sign of Madoc, they sent mes-
sengers in all directions to find news of him, but all they could
discover was that he had turned his footsteps homewards after
bidding farewell to his betrothed at Pen Craig Daf. All the
countryside turned out to find him, searching every place in
the countryside for miles around, and dragging every river,
but they couldn't find a trace of Madoc.

When many weeks of searching had gone by, Madoc's
parents sought the advice of an ancient hermit, Gweiryd,
who dwelt in a cave high up in the wilds, and asked him
when their lost son would return. 'He will never return
during your lifetimes,' said Gweiryd. 'The ancient judgement of the fairies on your house has fallen on Madoc's
shoulders. There is no hope for you. Your line is ended.'

Life drifted on like smoke in the wind. Weeks grew into
months and months into years, until gradually everyone
came to believe that the hermit Gweiryd had spoken the
truth. All except one person. Madoc's betrothed, Teleri, never
stopped believing with all her heart that her beloved was

alive and would return to her. Every morning when the sun rose above the horizon, Teleri would stand on the summit of a high rock, looking out over the landscape for her love. When the dusk of every day was falling, Teleri would be seen at the same spot, looking for some sign of Madoc until the sun sank behind the land of the west.

Madoc's father and mother died, and their bodies were laid to rest, but Teleri never lost hope. She watched for her love in all weathers, and in all seasons, year after long year until her bright eyes dimmed and her chestnut hair turned to silver; she went blind, and still she gazed for her love through sightless eyes. Finally death put an end to Teleri's long and worn-out hopes, and they buried her in the graveyard of the old Chapel of the Fan. One by one, everyone who had known Madoc died, and his strange disappearance became only a faint tradition.

Teleri never knew that her belief was true: Madoc was still alive, and this is what happened to him.

As Madoc was walking back to Pantannas from Pen Craig Daf, the sweetest music he had ever heard in his life came towards him from out of a cave in the Raven's Rift. Madoc was enchanted, and he stopped to listen. The music seemed to recede further into the cave after a while, and he stepped inside to hear better.

The melody retreated further and further, and Madoc, forgetting everything else but the magic of the music, followed it further and further into the recesses of the cavern. After he had been listening for an hour or two, the music suddenly stopped, leaving no sound but the dank dripping of water in the cave.

Madoc suddenly remembered everything, and realised that after the strange events of the night, his parents would be worried about his return. He retraced his footsteps rapidly to the mouth of the cave, where the sky was bright with sunlight already. Had he really been here all night? He must hurry!

He quickened his pace along the old road back towards Pantannas, and past the Fan Chapel – but there was no Fan Chapel there any more. Madoc wondered at this – how long had he been away? – and hurried faster towards Pantannas.

At last, here was Pantannas farmhouse. Madoc opened the door and went in. The place smelt unfamiliar. Sitting by the fire was an old, old man who woke up with a start. 'What! Who are you, marching into a stranger's house so boldly?'

Bewilderment overtook Madoc now. He looked around the farmhouse, and didn't recognise the furniture. He went to the kitchen window and looked out. There were walls and trees he didn't know: and yet this place was definitely his home. How could this be? He became dimly aware that some great change had happened to his life, and answered faintly, 'I am Madoc.'

'Madoc?' said the old man. 'Madoc? I don't know you. There is no Madoc living in this place, and I've never known anyone of that name. The only Madoc I have ever heard of was one who, my grandfather said, disappeared suddenly from this place, nobody knew where, many hundreds of years ago when the old family still used to live here.'

Madoc sank down on an unfamiliar chair and tears rolled down his cheeks. The old man's heart went out to him, and he got up and put a hand on Madoc's shoulder to comfort him. As soon as his hand touched the weeping figure, it crumbled into fine, dry dust.

7

Harvest and Home

Obbly, obbly-onker, my best conker,
Obbly, obbly-o, my best go …

Worcestershire

It's late September, the harvest is in, and the days and nights are equal once again. The summer is past, and the cooler air of autumn brings the first leaves twirling down to the ground. We are heading into the dark once more. Plants prepare for the winter through fruits and seeds, and through discarding what they don't need. The clearing-out begins.

LAZY LAWRENCE

The Celts called the apple the food of the gods, and through-out history the apple has been associated with love, beauty and abundance. Our domestic apple is descended from the wild crab-apple, and many 'wildings' (apple trees that have grown from the pips of domesticated varieties) occur in the British countryside and vary widely in their character.

In the Middle Ages, apple trees were deliberately planted in hedgerows around the common fields. The planting and tending of orchards, and work with the old local apple varieties, is a true craft. Traditionally, when apple-picking, the last apple is left on the tree for the Apple Tree Man, who ensures good harvests in the future.

No matter what the crop, there are stories of spirit guardians. Awd Goggie guards gooseberry bushes, sometimes in the form of a giant caterpillar. Melch Dick is a dwarf that guards unripe nut-trees (yes really!). The Colt-Pixy, or Lazy Lawrence, guards orchards. This story is from Dorset.

Lazy Lawrence is anything but lazy. They say he's a fine fairy colt, free and wild, green eyes flashing and a fine set of sharp teeth. If you've not been stealing, and you're in a safe place at a safe distance, and it's a full moon, you might glimpse Lazy Lawrence galloping around the orchards, guarding those precious apples.

But if you've been stealing? Those gnashers would make any boy drop the apples they'd been scrumping, and run for their lives, and they'd be right to, if they didn't want a nasty nip right in the breeches. No thief can escape the teeth and the hooves of Lazy Lawrence, and if you look into his green eyes, they'll transfix you, and you won't be able to move hand or foot. That's about the justice of it.

Lazy Lawrence, let me go.

Don't hold me summer and winter too.

A farmer's widow had two orchards left to her, with good cider apples and fine eaters and cookers. There were Buttery Doors, Warriors, Golden Balls and Melcombe Russet. Those apples would keep her in comfort all her days, if they were harvested and sold at Wareham market. But the old woman was getting on in years, with a blossomy head to her, and she needed help with the orchard. She'd always kept to the old ways, setting out a dish of cream and a pail of water at night, and so help she got. The help didn't come before it was needed, of course.

A dark-hearted conjurer lived nearby, and he took a fancy to the apples in the old woman's orchard, so he hatched a plan. He made a great apple-hamper, and he hid inside one night, and then he made it roll quietly into the orchard, and set still between the big old apple trees. Then he made a silent magic, and made all the apples in the orchard come down in a circle around that hamper.

The magic was stronger than he thought, and the apples came pelting down hard, not only around the hamper but into it as well, and straight on top of his head. He hadn't bargained for that, and when a nice big Warrior hit him right in the eye, fair blinding him, he yelled, 'OW!' and climbed up out of the hamper to get away from the danger. He fetched right up under the set of fine gnashers that belonged to Lazy Lawrence.

The conjurer hadn't bargained for that either. He was shown what happens to thieves who make spells, and then break them by shouting out of their turn. Round and round the orchard he was chased, well kicked, and nicely nipped, and so he tried to run in the other direction, and then he came face to face with those shining green eyes of the Colt-Pixy, and that stopped him altogether in his tracks.

The next morning at the crack of dawn, the old lady and her helpers came to the orchard for the harvest to take to market. But all the apples had been picked already. There they all were, in a gurt hamper, and in a big circle around it; and right in the middle, there was a conjuror rooted to the spot, covered in bruises and bites, all ghoulish like a crow-scarer, with a mess of one eye and a big shiner, and the other big scared eye swivelling round his head, unable to speak or move a muscle.

All the folk of the village came to see the conjuror trans-fixed there, and no one did anything – best not to free him too quickly – but they whispered and pointed to a ring of hoof-marks in the dew, that went all round the orchard, and they really enjoyed laughing for a good long time: 'Hey, old thief, has Lawrence got your legs?'

When the sun came up and got hot, the hoof-marks disappeared with the dew – and so did the conjuror, disappeared right into the next county he did. He only had one eye to see through, so he didn't get as far as he would like. Some say he's still running.

THE CROWS AND THE PEAR TREES

I first came across a Somerset version of this story about a magic cider apple tree, but I prefer this Gloucestershire one, adapted from H. J. Massingham's tale in Briggs' 'A Dictionary of British Folk Tales'. Bird-lime is a sticky substance used to trap wild birds, and its use is now illegal in the UK and Ireland.

When I was a young man, I was a carter, and in those days there was a good bit of carrying by road, in wagons and drays, up towards Gloucester.

I got to know that road pretty well, and in time I spied five handsome pear trees in the hedge alongside the road just outside Newent. The first time I saw them, they were in full flower, and a pretty enough sight and scent they were. Well, when it came to September, the trees were loaded with fruit, and so I whoad up my horses, and got me a pocketful of pears, and they were lovely – not mousey, not sleepy, but as soft as butter, and pretty moreish.

It seemed to me strange that any man could plant such desperately good pear trees in a hedge, and against the high road, so I asked a nearby innkeeper about it. This is the tale he told.

'Your pear trees were originally planted in a fine meadow up near Pershore, where the land is very good, and they had good bearings of fine fruit.

'But sadly for the farmer who owned them, there was a big rookery in some old elms nearby, and some jackdaws close by as well. As soon as the pears were ripe, those damned old crows would come and settle on the branches of the pear trees, and they'd peck and peck and peck, until they'd eaten all the fruit clean from the trees, and none for the farmer.

'When the next season came round, the farmer reckoned that he'd had enough of the old crows; so just before the pears were ripe enough, he took a can of bird-lime, and a long ladder, and gummed the bird-lime all over the branches of the trees.

'The next day was sunny, and the fruit starting to ripen in the warm. So caw! went one old crow, and caw-caw! went another, and then the whole hustle of them flew up and settled in the pear trees.

'Pretty soon there was a loud squawking and crawking because those old crows couldn't even move a foot, and they were stuck as fast as a rabbit in a snare, and they knew it.

'"Well then," said the farmer, "I've got them this time. I'll get my old gun, and shoot the lot of them," so off he went to fetch his gun.

'Now crows aren't stupid, and they heard what he said, and set up caw-cawing and flapping their wings fit to bust; but as soon as they saw the farmer come back with his gun, they all set off with such a huge and desperate flapping that up came all five pear trees by the roots, out of the good earth, and whiffley-whiffley-whiffley, off they flew, pear trees and all, towards Tewkesbury and over the river Severn.

'After they'd been flying a while, there came a smartish shower of rain, and that washed most of the bird-lime away, and clunk, clunk, clunk, clunk, clunk, down dropped the pear trees into a hedge by the high roadway, towards Newent – took good root they did, and there they are now.

'But I'm damned if I know what happened to the old crows afterwards, or if they ever ate pears again.'

THE FARMER AND THE BOGGART

Boggarts, or bogles, are creatures bent on causing havoc, often linked with the land. They are usually ugly, uncouth, and annoyingly persistent in their efforts, and should be avoided where possible, although they are not evil, only troublemak-ers. They have a nasty habit of hanging round potato fields, causing blight.

Potatoes have caused a lot of grief since they were brought here by Francis Drake in the late 1500s. Did you know that potatoes once fetched £300 a pound as an aphrodisiac? And that in Ireland, a kettle of boiled potatoes, buried on an enemy's land, ruins his crop?

The farmer in this story, faced with threats and then bargaining from a boggart, was much craftier. A similar story can be found in many places across England and Scotland.

Farmer Joe had just got himself a new field, and he was pleased with it. He'd got himself a good price, he had signed all the paperwork, and now, on a fresh spring day, he'd done a fine job of ploughing it.

Joe stood and looked at the newly ploughed field, the fine soil and the possibilities, and thought about what he should plant this year.

That's when the voice said: 'Hoi! This is my land!'

Joe looked around and saw no one: then he looked down, and there was a boggart, squat and hairy and ugly as you like, strong as a six-year-old horse, and with arms almost as long as tackle-poles.

'This is my land!' the boggart insisted. 'You're trespassing. Go somewhere else.'

'But I've just ploughed it,' said Joe.

'That's your problem.'

'I've got all the paperwork.'

'Paperwork means nothing to me, I'm a boggart.'

'I can take you to court.'

'I'll have nothing to do with the law. They've never shown me justice. Now get off my land!'

Joe scratched his head and wondered what to do.

'Very well,' he said, 'let's reach a compromise, let's go half and half. Why don't we share the harvest from this field? You can take what grows above the ground, or you can take what grows beneath the ground, and I will take the other. Can't say fairer than that. Only, mind, you stick to what you settle, and keep your word; I don't want no back-reckonings after.'

'I'll take what grows above the ground,' said the boggart. 'Done.'

They shook hands on it. The boggart's handshake was black and slimy.

Well, that settled Farmer Joe's mind on what to grow that year: he decided to grow potatoes. Of course, when the boggart came along at harvest-time, Joe had a whole haul of potatoes from below ground, but all the boggart got was the helms and twitch. He was in a sore temper about it, I can tell you.

'This is my land, and I want my proper share of the crop,' said the boggart. 'Next year, then, *I* will take all that grows below ground.'

'Done,' said Joe, and there was another slimy handshake.

The next spring, Joe sowed the field with wheat. When the boggart came around again at the harvest-time, Jo got all the corn and the straw, and nothing was left for the boggart but stubble and thin roots. The boggart was hopping up and down in anger, but he couldn't do anything about it as the farmer had kept his word.

'Look,' said the boggart. 'I know your game. Here's my proposal, for MY land. You sow wheat again next spring-time, and when it comes around to harvest again, we should cut the crop together, and each of us take what he cuts.'

'Done,' said Joe. There was another, slightly more violent, slimy handshake from the boggart.

After the boggart had disappeared, grumbling, Joe consulted the local cunning man of the village. On his advice, Joe got a large number of thin iron rods made by the local blacksmith, and put them into the boggart's side of the wheat crop before it was tall. When the wheat had grown up and turned to gold, you wouldn't have known there were any iron rods at all.

Harvest came around, and there were Farmer Joe and the boggart at opposite ends of the field, both scything the wheat as fast and as close as they could. Joe was getting on well, but the boggart's strength was failing; he was stopping, and starting, and cursing, and great chunks were being bitten out of the blade of his scythe. So the boggart stopped to rest, but Joe kept on cutting and kept on cutting, until he had nearly come over to the boggart's side of the field. At last the boggart threw his scythe down in despair, and cried, 'Take your mucky old land; I'll have no more to do with it.'

And off the boggart went, never to come back. At least, he didn't come back to the fields, but he went to the lanes, and scared people out at night on their own; and if you leave your dinner, or your tools, lying around, watch out, because he might make off with them.

HARVEST DAFTNESS

Here are two very silly harvest stories, the first from Cumberland and the second from Sussex.

A crop of turnips was grown some years ago, by Clem Mossop of Prior Skeae, near Co'der Brig. The soil is grand there, and combined with heavy mucking and wide thinning out, Clem raised such turnips as you never heard tell of before or since – they were massive. Folk visited from far away to look at them.

At about Martinmas, a young bull fairly ate his way into one of these turnips until he was right inside it, and he stayed there quite happy. They thought the beast was lost until a while after Christmas, when he walked out of the turnip a good bit fatter than when he went in.

Clem was so pleased, he had the shell of the same turnip carried up to the farmhouse, and put some long sticks across it for perches, and it made a brilliant hen house – the hens sat in it at night.

Sadly it wasn't to last, and the next winter, the turnip finally softened and fell together after a hard frost.

*

Meanwhile, much further south, and many years ago, two fellows came down from London – now everyone knows that's a place where all the men are wise as owls.

They met an old Sussex man who was toddling along the road near his village, with a pumpkin under his arm. The two London chaps had never seen the likes of a pumpkin before, and didn't know what it was. So one said to the other, 'Let's see what this old fellow's got under his arm.'

'Good morning, mister,' said one of them to the old man.

'Good morning,' said the old chap, all friendly.

'What's that under your arm?' said the Londoners.

'That'll be a mare's egg, then,' said the old man.

'Is that so?' said the Londoners, believing him like lambs. 'We've never seen such a good one before.'

'Yes,' said the old chap. 'There's a lot of common mares' eggs around, but this one's a thoroughbred, and that's why it's so fine.'

The Londoners' eyes were like saucers. 'Will you sell it?'

'Well,' said the old chap, hesitating slightly. 'I don't mind selling it, but I doubt you would give me what I wanted for it; I've a mind to take no less than a sovereign for this here thoroughbred mare's egg.'

So after much talk these London chaps gave the man a bright sovereign, and so he gave them the pumpkin, looking all wistful about it, and he said:

'Mind you carry it carefully, for it'll hatch soon, I reckon.'

'All right,' said the Londoners, 'we'll be careful.'

So off they went over the fields with the mare's egg. Presently, the one who was carrying it caught his foot in a hole in the ground and he dropped the pumpkin all of a sudden, and it cracked open. This started a hare from the bushes, and the hare ran down the hill, and the Londoners were sure that it was their baby colt, and so they shouted out to some men working at the bottom of the hill, 'Hie! Stop our colt! Stop our colt!'

But it was never caught.

TWO MOONS IN MAY

This Somerset story tells of our dependency on plants. The conditions aren't always good, and the harvest doesn't always succeed.

A dear old couple, Sammy and Nanny, had lived on their little farm since anyone could remember. They had an acre of hay, an acre of corn, and a little vegetable patch. They kept a cow and a pig, and five hens. They worked their land the old-fashioned way, and foraged for blackberries and whortleberries when the seasons changed. Every night, they would tell the happenings of the day to the old elm tree at the bottom of the field. Then, before locking up, they'd leave out a dish of cream, and it would be licked clean by the morning.

Sammy and Nanny also had an old donkey that carried the panniers to market twice a week. They only sold bits and pieces – some eggs, butter, vegetables, berries and apples – but the quality of their knitting was famous, and people always bought their stockings, so they just about scraped by.

Sammy liked to look at the night skies, peppered with bright stars and garlanded with the Milky Way. One May Day night, Sammy looked up and said, 'There's a full moon up there. There's another full moon later this month as well.'

'That's bad news,' said Nanny. 'You know what they say: "Two moons in May, no corn, no hay." But we'll be all right, somehow.'

The weather that spring was terrible, and it didn't get any better for the summer. Most of the hay went black, and the poor stuff that didn't had to be hung on the fences to dry, and any corn that was harvested sprouted in all the rain. There were no plums or apples, the blackberries went mouldy, and the sow only had five piglets.

So Sammy and Nanny knitted for all they were worth just to get money to buy food. Still it rained, and by September they ran out of money to buy more wool. Rent day was coming; they'd sold the hens and the pigs, and they still didn't have enough. And still it rained.

Sammy was standing by the old fireplace, with barely enough fire in the grate to shift the damp. 'There's nothing for it,' he said. 'We'll have to sell the old donkey, and the cow and the calf. Otherwise we'll never make it through the winter.'

Nanny sat and cried. 'There'll be no dish of cream to set out at night, the first time all our married lives. Then things will never get better.'

'I'll go up to the old spring and fetch them some cold water instead,' said Sammy. 'I'll tell the old elm tree. They'll know then, and maybe they'll not cause us harm.'

Next morning, Nanny milked the cow for the last time and brushed the donkey, and then with tearful farewells Sammy took them up to the market. He came home empty-handed apart from a few coins in his pocket, to a very quiet farm.

'Did you get enough to cover the rent for the winter?' said Nanny.

'If we're careful, yes,' said Sammy.

Then Sammy picked up a jug and went out to find the old spring. He'd got there, made a prayer, filled up the jug with cool, clear water, and was making his way home, when he saw three bags lying in the middle of the road. One was made of blue velvet stuff, and very full, and when Sammy picked it up, it clinked and chinked with coin. The red flaxen bag was smaller and half-full with coin, and the smallest was a pretty green silk bag, flat and empty. All the bags were sealed tight with cord.

Sammy looked around. There was no one there. Somebody must be missing these bags, somebody would want them back. He gathered all three bags together and took them to show Nanny.

Nanny had already gone to bed upset; so Sammy went up to the old elm tree and told it everything that had

happened. He went back to the cottage, put a dish with the last of the cream and a dish of cold spring water outside, and then hid the three bags in the thatch roof of the little cottage until they could be claimed by whoever had lost them.

Next day, when he walked up to market, Sammy had the crier call about the three lost bags of market money. Plenty of people tried to claim them; but Sammy had devised a clever question about the bags and nobody got it right. So he walked back home again.

Then came along Old Sal Slack, the local cunning woman. 'The bags are mine.'

'What's the words written on them, then, Sal?'

'Harum Scarum.'

'Out you go,' they said, and showed her down the road.

And then a poacher came calling and claimed the bags were his, but he said the words on the bags were 'Money Bags', so he was shown down the road too.

And then, as Sammy and Nanny were sitting sadly in the gloom by their poor excuse for a fire, a fine-looking stranger in green poked his head around the kitchen door. 'I want my bags,' said he and smiled at them. They felt better at once, but they had to ask the question: 'What's written on the bags, then?' 'Why, nothing at all,' came the reply, and they knew he was the right one.

The stranger smiled at them again. 'Sammy and Nanny, I know I can trust you. I'll leave the bags with you tonight, because you put cream out last night too, and went without, and I'll be along to see your landlord about the rent in the morning.'

Next morning there was the stranger in green, still smiling.

'Give me the three bags, go out for a good walk, and don't come back until the sun is over the top of the old elm tree.'

They took the stranger's advice, and as soon as Sammy and Nanny were out of sight, the stranger in green sat outside the little cottage on a bench, and he put the three bags out in a row beside him.

Then the landlord rode by on an old nag. 'I've come for my rent, and the farm too; that old couple will never make it through the winter,' he said. The stranger in green just smiled and pointed to the fat blue velvet bag that clinked. 'There's your rent,' he said. 'Just count it.' The landlord counted the gold, although there were a few gold pieces at the bottom of the bag he somehow forgot to count. 'That's just about right,' he said, and tried to hurry away – but not before the stranger in green had insisted on full receipt for the year's rent and the farm.

Then the parson came riding by on a fine hunting cob. 'I've come for my tithes,' he said, and he took the red linen bag – but he had to sign a receipt too.

When the sun was over the top of the old elm tree, Sammy and Nanny returned, and there was the stranger in green still sitting on the bench, still smiling. 'Here's your receipts, and the little green bag for you both,' he said. 'No one has claimed it today. And don't forget the cream tonight.' Then the clouds broke and the last light from the sunset broke through and shone on them, as if it were the first sunlight they had seen all year; and in the sunlight the stranger in green disappeared before Sammy and Nanny could say so much as a 'thank you'.

'Well, that's kindness itself. We'll get by now,' said Nanny, 'but there's no cream for tonight! We might sell the little green bag – it's empty, but it's pretty.' She felt the silken cloth, and there inside the linking was the shape of a coin; and when Nanny managed to get it out of the lining, it was a whole golden guinea.

Sammy and Nanny went back into their farmhouse, and there out in the yard was the old donkey and the pigs and hens, and there down in the field was their cow and calf, as if they'd never gone away. They had something to eat that night and a good fire and when they went to hide the bag away safely, there was another golden guinea in the lining. The green silk bag never seemed to be empty after that.

When the landlord got home with his blue chinking velvet bag of spoils, he opened it up and found nothing but yellowing, dried moss. When the parson came back from his service the next morning, the red linen bag on his desk was nothing more than a small charred pile of ash.

As for Sammy and Nanny, they did very well after that. And there was always a dish of cream left outside the door at night, and by morning it was always licked clean.

KATE CRACKERNUTS

Hazel is a mercurial tree, the ancient Celtic tree of knowledge, and in the south west they say that silver snakes twine around its roots. Hazel can be used to divine for water, and can even invoke invisibility. Throughout the islands, hazelnuts were believed to be receptacles of wisdom, even the food of the gods. They could cure fevers and coughs, and clear the head (these days, you would be forgiven for thinking that grey squirrels must carry an awful lot of wisdom, and never be troubled with illness – but they haven't quite got the knack of invisibility yet).

This story was originally collected in Orkney. Hazel was once common in Scotland, and the name Caledonia comes from Cal Dun, *meaning 'hill of hazel'. The motif of going away with the fairies and dancing all night to exhaustion, to be an invalid by day, occurs in a number of fairy tales, and is thought to refer to the symptoms of tuberculosis.*

Once upon a time there was a king and a queen, and they each had a daughter. The daughters cared a great deal for each other, but the queen was jealous that the king's daughter was more beautiful than her own, and she determined to do something about it. She asked the advice of the local henwife, who told her to send the girl to her house the following morning, before she had eaten anything.

So the beautiful princess was sent off to the henwife's house the following morning before breakfast, to fetch some eggs. The girl had smuggled a piece of bread in her pocket and ate as she walked, and when she got to the henwife's house she asked for the eggs. The henwife said 'Surely; just lift the lid of that pot over there, and see.' The girl did so, and nothing happened. 'Get home to your mother, and tell her to keep the kitchen door tighter shut!' said the henwife.

The queen knew from this that the girl had had something to eat, and so she watched her the next morning, and sent her away fasting to fetch the eggs. But the princess met some country folk shelling peas by the roadside, and she spoke to them and was given a handful of peas, which she ate along the way. So the same thing – nothing – happened at the henwife's house.

On the third day, the queen was quite determined, and so she made sure the girl was fasting and went along to the henwife's house with her. Now, when the girl lifted the lid off the pot, off jumped the princess's own pretty head, and on to the princess's neck jumped a sheep's head. And the sheep's weird eyes swivelled round to look at the queen and the henwife mournfully, but the sheep could not speak.

The queen, now satisfied, returned home with the changed princess. But the queen's own daughter, Kate, took a fine linen cloth and wrapped it around her sister's head. She took her by the hand and they both left the castle and went out to seek their fortune.

They walked and they walked and they walked, right out of their parents' kingdom and into another, until they reached the castle of another king. This king had two sons, one of whom was well and one very sick.

'That's strange,' said Kate to the king, 'for we are both princesses, one of us well, and my sister here very sick, as you can see. Can we stay here for the night?'

'On one condition,' said the king. 'You must stay up all night to watch over my sick son, for I fear he is very unwell. If all is not well in the morning, then your life will be forfeit, for my son is precious to me.'

Kate went into the room where the prince was lying in bed, feverish and drifting in and out of consciousness. She took one look at his face and knew that she could love this man – if he lived. She stayed by his bedside and listened to his rasping breaths.

Until midnight, all was peaceful. But as the clock struck midnight, the prince got out of bed, as if in a trance. He dressed himself, pulled on his boots and walked downstairs. Kate followed behind him, unnoticed. The prince went to the stable, saddled his horse, called his hound, and jumped into the saddle. Kate leapt up lightly behind him and put her arms around his waist. He gave no signal that he knew she was there.

Away rode the prince and Kate through the greenwood, with the prince's hound running swiftly beside them. As they passed hazel trees, Kate plucked hazelnuts from the trees and filled her apron with them. They rode on and on until they came to a green hill in the middle of a clearing. The prince here drew his bridle and spoke: 'Open, open, green hill, and let the young prince in with his horse and hound.' Kate added quickly: 'His lady behind him.'

Immediately the green hill opened and they went inside. There was a magnificent hall, brightly lit, and many beautiful ladies surrounded the prince and led him off to the dance, while Kate, unnoticed, sat by the door. She watched all night as the prince danced and danced and danced with the fairies, with seemingly endless energy, and not a trace of sickness. Kate tried not to feel jealous, but she kept watching over him.

Eventually the cock crew with the dawn, and the prince hurried to get back on horseback. Kate jumped up behind, and they rode home, and the prince undressed and collapsed exhausted into bed. While he slept, Kate sat down by the fire, cracked the hazelnuts and ate them. When the household wakened, the king came into the prince's chamber and saw him sleeping soundly.

'He's had a good night, I tell no word of a lie,' said Kate from the fireside, and she grinned. The king was delighted. 'I would be willing to sit up for another night and watch him, if it pleases you,' she said.

'Yes,' said the king. 'There will be a bag of silver as a reward if all is well in the morning; but if all is not well, then your life will be forfeit, remember.'

The second night passed as the first one had done. As the prince was dancing with the fairies, and she sat beside the door unnoticed, Kate saw a chubby fairy child playing with a wand on the floor close by. One of the fairies said, 'Three strikes of that wand would make Kate's sister as bonnie as ever she was.' So Kate rolled some of her hazelnuts towards the child, until he let the wand fall to pick them up, and she took the wand and put it in her apron.

When Kate got back to the castle with the prince, and made sure he was safely sleeping, she went to find her sister, who was also asleep. Kate used the wand to make the sheep's head disappear, and transform it back into the head of the beautiful princess. Her sister had a wonderful surprise when she looked in the mirror the following morning; and she went to find the other brother.

Meanwhile, Kate asked the king for a third night over-seeing the sick prince. 'Very well,' said the king. 'This time there will be a bag of gold as a reward if all is well in the morning; but if all is not well, then you will lose your life, so guard him well.'

'I would like nothing more than for him to restore to full health,' said Kate. 'If he does, may I marry him?'

The king agreed. He had taken a shine to Kate, and could see how much she cared for his son.

The same thing happened on the third night: another ride through the greenwood, and more hazelnuts, and another fairy dance, with Kate waiting by the door. There, again, was the chubby little fairy child, and this time he was playing with a small brown bird. Kate heard one of the fairies say, 'Three bites of that little bird would make the sick prince well again.' Kate rolled hazelnuts over to the little child until he picked them up and dropped the bird. Kate picked up the bird and put it into her apron.

At cockcrow they set off again, back to the castle, with the prince exhausted. As soon as he was safely sleeping, Kate went to the fireside, took out the little bird, plucked its feathers and cooked it carefully over the fire. Soon, there was a very savoury smell of roasted bird in the room, and the prince woke up.

'Oh!' said the sick prince, 'I wish I could have a bite of that bird.' So Kate gave him a bit of the bird to eat, and some colour came back to his face, and he rose up on his elbow. A little while later he cried out again, 'Oh, if I could have another bite of that bird!' So Kate gave him another bit to eat, and he sat up against his pillows, and sparkle came back into his eyes. Then he said again, 'Oh! If I could have a third bite of that bird!' So Kate gave him a third bit to eat, and he rose quite well, dressed himself, and sat down by the fire. When the king came in the morning he found Kate and the prince sitting by the fire, cracking hazelnuts and cracking jokes.

That is how the sick prince married the well princess, and the well prince married the sick princess, and they all lived happy and died happy.

8

THE TURNING OF THE WHEEL

Old sins do come up again like weeds
after a shower.

Somerset

By the end of October, the darkness has returned. Long before the commercialism of Hallowe'en, the old festival of All Hallows, or Samhain, celebrated the end of the old year and the 'thin veil between the worlds' of the earth and the supernatural. This is a time of death, decay and breakdown. The plant world has prepared for the new beginnings of next year, and only those evergreen plants like holly, ivy and yew remain green.

THE ELDER-TREE WITCH

Elder is gloriously and unapologetically witchy. Its blossoms are fragrant and scent the midsummer, but the berries and the wood are not to be messed with. Many people used to believe that elder trees and witches were one and the same thing, and for this reason kept elder out of their hedgerows. Here's the story of a Somerset farmer who was a little bit careless in that regard.

There was a farm close to Knighton, and it's not good land round there, but the farmer did his best with it. He had a few cows and they gave fine milk. There weren't any woods on the farm, but there were good stout hedges, and the farmer was glad they had no elder in them. Everyone knew that if you tried to chop an elder tree down, it would turn into a witch who would chase you until you crossed running water; and he didn't like the sound of that.

But there came a time when someone, or something, was stealing milk from the farmer's cows.

He couldn't afford the loss, so he got up during the night to go and check on the cows, and to spy on anyone who was stealing.

He went up to the top field, and there was a shadow of a small tree up by the hedge, a tree that he didn't remember being there. A gangly, dark tree. An elder tree.

The farmer was all in a cold sweat, and he drove the cows into the little home pasture, but the chain was gone from the gate and he couldn't fasten it; so he used a big stone against it to keep it shut.

Later on, he told his wife and daughter what he'd seen.

'You gurt fool!' said his wife. 'Did you draw a cross in the mud, this side of the gate?'

No, he hadn't.

The daughter was at the window, and she went pale as a ghost. 'It's out in the pasture, out there right now among the cows. It's an elder tree!' She started shrieking and running round the house closing all the shutters.

The old granny in the corner by the fire sat and listened and said nothing. She laid a big iron shovel among the red-hot embers, and raked in a faggot of ashwood to burn well.

The farmer was a brave man, and his cows were important to him. He puffed out his chest. 'Wife, go and fetch the silver button that came off my Sunday coat.'

She'd sewn it back on, but she snipped off the button and brought it to him, and by the time he had loaded his gun with the button his daughter had swung the cross-bar down against the back door, and the granny had got the iron shovel nice and hot.

Then the wife opened the front door of the farmhouse a crack, and the farmer looked out. There was the tree in among his cows, so he couldn't take a long shot for fear of hitting one of them.

'I'll have to go out there,' he said. 'Hold the door open and let me out and in again if I have to run for it.'

Out he went, trembling all over, to save his cows. He had to get too close for comfort to take aim, and he couldn't keep the gun steady. The silver button missed by a long way.

The tree yelled out, and so did the farmer, and she leapt after him, and he leapt too, and she came rushing after him and he ran towards the door as quick as he could. He didn't do badly for a man of his circumference, and his wife slammed the door shut so quickly she caught his coat-tails in it, but she managed to drop the iron bar down. And there they all were inside the house.

They could hear the tree's branches scraping and rattling outside and the tree shrieking like a high gale, but she couldn't get in, trouble the doors and windows as she might. The wife and daughter were shrieking as well, and the farmer bellowed like a bull-calf trying to get his coat-tails free and be out to his cows again. He had the courage, but not the right knowledge.

The old granny was quiet. She got up from the hearth with a gurt shovel of burning coals and she said to the daughter, 'Open the back door wide,' and the girl did. When the elder tree came at the back door shrieking and leaping, the granny threw the red-hot coals all over her and then calmly shut the door, and they all saw the blue flames, bleeding twigs and crackling tree through the window. And there was no more shrieking after that.

After a while, granny took the ash cattle-prod and went outside. The heap of ashes was cold already, and she made a criss-cross in the ashes with the ash stick. The farmer could now free his coat-tails and go out to see the cows.

Then the neighbours all came, and there was celebration, for they said that was the end of Madam Widecombe the witch; but it wasn't to be – they found out she was still around, and so was the old black witch over at Steart. Then someone told them that old Raggy Lyddy at Doddington had been burned to death – so that's who it was.

THE WONDERFUL WOOD

A number of stories tell of trees protecting the vulnerable, and even dealing out justice to the wicked. This story comes from Warwickshire.

Once upon a time, and it wasn't your time and it wasn't my time but it was a very good time, there was a cruel king who liked to ride out hunting not the stag, not the boar, but the young maiden. After he caught a maiden (and had his wicked way with her) he would kill her by using his sharp sword to cut off her head.

Because he was the king, nobody could do anything to stop this wicked man finding his twisted pleasure, and he terrorised the countryside for miles around. All the fathers and mothers sent their daughters away to safety if they could, but there was one little maid in a lonely cottage who couldn't go. She lived with her grandmother, who was too poor to send her away, so she kept the maid well hidden, and earned their bread and keep by spinning.

Now there was a great wild wood near the cottage and nobody dared go into it, not even the wicked king, because of the great and powerful oak tree that grew there and ruled the place. It was a place for trees, not humans.

One market day the grandmother was very ill, so the little maid had to take along the hanks of wool to market or they'd starve. Well, the little maid cried, and her grandmother cried too and blessed her and told her to be as quiet as possible, and not to go through the great wild wood although it was the quickest way. The little maid took heed of all the advice, and off she went on her tiptoes to market carrying the bundle of wool.

She hadn't got far when she caught sight of the cruel king riding along in the distance. She didn't run, but quietly, very quietly, she tiptoed straight into the great wild wood.

Immediately she felt safer. It was a wonderful wood. She walked for some time in the direction of the market, and there in a clearing in the middle of the wonderful wood was a huge oak tree. This must be the great oak! The little maid wasn't scared. She curtsied politely to the tree, and asked if she could travel through safely, and the tree let her go past, and through the wood into the town to market. But the cruel king had seen her flit through the trees, and that wasn't all right. He spurred his horse and he rode after her, into the great wild wood.

When the king got to the huge oak tree, he cursed at it, and tried to push his horse through past the tree. It just happened that a large bough fell from the oak tree at that very moment, it fell heavy and it broke the king's neck. There he fell on the ground, stone dead, and his horse rode away terrified.

So that was all right. But the king's men came looking for him. They could see him through the trees. They galloped into the wood to cut the great oak tree down in revenge.

The tree gave a great, creaking groan, a call to his own kind thereabouts. As the men readied themselves with axes under its boughs, the other trees drew in closer, and closer, and loomed in on them, until there was nothing left but a tree three times the size of the old oak tree with branches in all directions, and no trace of the men left. It was a wonderful wood. It was a place for trees, not humans.

JUDGE POPHAM'S OAK

Trees are often associated with historical figures, and here's an intriguing example.

Sir John Popham was born in 1531, the son of a Bridgwater MP; his mother came from St Donat's Castle in Glamorgan (an easy journey from Bridgwater by boat in those days). Popham rose to become Lord Chief Justice of England, and a wealthy landowner with his main residence at Wellington, Somerset. He was involved in the trial of Mary, Queen of Scots (1587) and presided over the trials of Sir Walter Raleigh (1603) and Guy Fawkes (1606).

For commoners in Elizabethan and early Stuart England, stealing pretty much anything (even food if you were starving) resulted in the death penalty by hanging. Popham's severity towards thieves was well known, and he was clearly disliked and feared by the people of Somerset. He died on 10 June 1607.

Wilscum Bottom is a gully to the west of the Wellington Monument, in the Blackdown Hills. A 'conjurer' is the local name for a white witch or hedge-witch.

Sir John Popham, the Hanging Judge, was thrown from his horse and broke his neck in Wilscum Bottom, that place with a pit that leads directly down to hell. After he died an oak tree grew up there containing his spirit, and the whole place went bad. It was so dangerous around there that the good people of Wellington decided to do something about it, and lay his ghost.

They sent for a conjurer from Waterrow to give them advice. He told them that the bad oak had to be uprooted and burned. So they fetched a lot of people and horses and they looped chains of iron around the oak tree. They covered up their ears in case the tree should scream, and the horses started to strain.

It didn't work. Those strong iron chains snapped like twigs, and everyone ran away as fast as their legs could carry them. Three blacksmiths were called (for luck) to mend the chains, but nobody would take on the challenge again; until one well-respected old ploughman said that if he were given ten oxen, he would be able to pull out the tree. He said he had seen the oxen kneeling on Christmas Eve, and knew they would be protected.

He took the oxen, but everyone else kept well away. The old ploughman took a Bible in his pocket and started bellowing out the psalms with all the practice of a lifetime in Wellington church, so loudly that they could be heard all the way to Wiveliscombe. He wound the chains around the oak, then he called out to the oxen and the oak tree came out of the ground as easily as a carrot. When it came out, there was a piercing scream from the tree that rang round the hills, but

the ploughman came out of it safe from harm, and so did the cattle. Everyone else covered their ears.

Popham's ghost got out of the tree somehow, before it was burned, and it hid in the woods below Wellington Hill, but it was so shaken that it didn't trouble anyone for years.

They put Popham's name on his wife Amy's grave, but his body does not lie there. Local people say that every New Year's Eve his ghost comes out of Popham's Pit (Wilscum Bottom) and takes one cock's step nearer to the grave. Until he has reached it, his soul will not rest in peace.

THE SPECTRE BRIDEGROOM

Hemp is originally from India, but it has been grown as a crop in the British Isles for over two thousand years, with records of it being grown in every county and country. Hemp is six times as strong as cotton and much more resistant to wear. In the sixteenth century, Henry VIII ordered that every farm over sixty acres should sow at least a quarter of an acre of hemp. It was mainly grown for fibre used to make ropes, fishing nets, clothes and paper, and hemp oil was burned in lamps.

There are historical records of hemp workers complaining of lightheadedness and headaches. The strain of hemp called marijuana (used as a recreational drug) has high levels of a substance called tetrahydrocannabinol (THC), and this led to its ban as a crop in the twentieth century; however, recent research has encouraged low-THC hemp to be grown again, as a sustainable and versatile crop with a low environmental footprint.

Hemp was also considered to be a raiser of spectres; the practice of using hemp seed for divination is recorded in many places. This story comes from Penwith in Cornwall.

Nancy Trenoweth was a maidservant up at the big house at Boscean. Her mother was well respected in the village for her religious ways and sensible nature, and Nancy had her mother's talents as well as being pretty and intelligent. Everyone loved Nancy, from the lowliest servant to the great farmer and his wife who hired her.

But Nancy did the thing you should never do: she fell in love with the son of the master of the house. His name was Frank Lenine, and he was very used to getting his own way with everything. Frank was living at home with plenty of opportunity to steal away with Nancy for secret time together. It was the worst-kept secret in the house.

When Frank's parents inevitably found out, and then learned that Frank wanted to marry Nancy, they were completely against the idea. 'It's preposterous,' said Frank's father. 'It will degrade the family for my only son to marry a common maidservant, no matter how sweet she is.' Nancy was sent away from the big house and Frank's father forbade them ever to meet again.

Of course, Frank and Nancy didn't listen. Every evening they would meet, sometimes in the woods, sometimes at the holy well, and once at night they even climbed the granite-pile at Treryn, and by the Logan Rock. And eventually, after several months of secret meetings, Nancy's waist began to swell and it was clear that she was carrying Frank's child.

Well, Nancy's parents insisted that he should honour their daughter and marry her, but Frank's father was obstinate. He took his son away to Plymouth, where Frank decided to escape from his father's tyranny and got a job on a ship to India. He didn't know how to write, so could send no word to his love; but she waited for him with her baby at her parents' house, sure that, wherever Frank was, he was thinking of her and that no distance could separate their souls. Who knows what Frank was feeling for Nancy during those long years.

When three years had passed, at Hallowe'en, two village girls persuaded Nancy to go with them to sow hemp seed in the churchyard. Nancy, who was the bravest of them, went first. She walked around the church nine times, and then threw hemp seed behind her on to the ground, repeating three times:

> Hemp seed I sow,
> Hemp seed I grow;
> For my true love to come after and mow.

Nancy then jumped forward and looked back over her shoulder, and there was Frank, scything hemp plants. But he looked angry, so angry that she cried out and broke the spell, and Frank vanished.

The next girl to sow hemp seed looked behind her and only saw a white coffin. All three of them shrieked and ran out of the churchyard and home, to trembling fear and troubled dreams.

November followed, and a few days later there was a terrible storm. A ship was wrecked on the rocks at Bernowhall Cliff, some way away from where Nancy lived. And on that ship was Frank Lenine. He was dragged from the water, but didn't survive the night. He lived long enough to beg the bystanders to send for Nancy, so that he might marry her before he died. But there was no time. He was buried in the local churchyard that day, before Nancy ever got to hear of his death.

That evening, still innocent of the tragedy, Nancy was looking out of the door into the dark night before locking up, when a horseman rode up and called her name. She knew the colt and she knew the voice: it was Frank! He told her that he had come to carry her away and make her his bride, so she sprang on to the horse and took his hand, hardly believing that her true love had come back to claim her. As she touched his clammy cold skin and grasped his waist to steady herself, Nancy became icy cold and stiff, and she couldn't speak. The rider galloped into the night for miles and miles, and as the horse dashed through a river, in the moonlight Nancy saw in the water the reflection of a shroud and grave-clothes on the figure of Frank, and she knew that she was being carried away by a spirit.

At last they passed a smithy, and Nancy's speech returned. 'Save me, save me!' she cried, and the smith ran out with a red-hot iron in his hand, caught her dress, and pulled her to the ground. But the spirit also held fast to Nancy's dress, and Nancy and the smith were dragged across the ground by the spirit and his horse over to the old almshouses near the churchyard. There the horse stopped, and there was a struggle. The smith used his iron to burn off the dress from the spirit rider's hand, and he carried Nancy back to the smithy. The spirit rider vanished into the churchyard wall.

The smith took Nancy home to her parents' house, but she died before morning. On Frank's grave they found the piece of cloth burned from Nancy's dress, which had been grasped in the rider's hand. They buried poor Nancy in Frank's grave. The girl who had seen the coffin also died within the year.

One of the sailors who survived the shipwreck later told a curious tale. On the night of 31 October, when they were at sea, Frank had fallen into a trance. When he recovered he said that he had been drawn out of his body by a spell, back to his old village, and nearly died in the process; and if he ever caught the woman who had done it and married her, he vowed to make her suffer the longest day she had to live, for what she had done to him.

So perhaps Frank hadn't been so faithful, after all.

DONALD AND THE WITCHES

Rowan trees used to be planted next to houses to protect them from witches and dark forces. The wood of the rowan was the part considered to hold protective powers. On the Isle of Man, rowan is still used together with primroses on May Eve for these reasons. This cautionary tale is from the Lake District. Kelpies are shape-shifting water spirits, often preying on humans and taking the shape of a horse. Again, we are reminded never to name fairies and never to give them thanks, for they don't like it and won't help again.

Donald finished his morning porridge and got up from the kitchen table. He had a long ride ahead of him, out to the moor to collect the sheep and bring them to the stone shelter of the fold, before the weather was set to grow wild and dangerous.

Donald's wife, Janet, gave him his plaid and crook and bonnet with a blessing laid on each, ready prepared. Donald saw the sprig of rowan berries in his bonnet, and his crook made of pale rowan wood, and he knew better than to speak anything of it. When he went outside to the autumn morning, Janet had hung branches of rowan berries between the pony's ears, tied more to his bridle, and Cu the sheep-dog was wearing a twisted collar of rowan twigs. She was clearly worried.

Donald, his pony and Cu the sheepdog set off for the moor, with Janet calling down a blessing of protection on them. 'We'll need that out there, the three of us,' said Donald.

When they passed through the village, the witchwives took stock of the situation and quickly closed their doors. Then they got out their blackthorn brooms and plotted. 'We'll just let him be, 'til he's over at Roaring Brig,' they said to one another. 'The kelpie is out today, and roaring for stormy weather, and she'll wash all his fairy charms away, and then we can get to work.'

It was a long way and a cold way and a dark way to the Roaring Brig, but Donald travelled steadily, and when he got there, they crossed the water at the safest place possible. The waters rose and swirled about them. The kelpie saw the pony's rowan bridle and Donald's charmed bonnet, but she didn't see the pale twiggy collar under Cu's ruff of fur.

Cu was swimming when the kelpie attacked, and he snarled and bit with strong teeth. The kelpie wailed and roared loudly and backed off. This wasn't what she had expected – no souls to feast on, and a bitten flank! Donald, his pony and Cu climbed out of the flooded burn, wet to the bone, and travelled steadily on, warmed by Janet's porridge and her blessings.

It was a long way and a cold way and a dark way to the high moor. Night fell to pitch black, and the crescent moon was almost blotted out by a coven of witches on blackthorn broomsticks, filling the air with their cackles. A violent gale whipped up around the travellers. Although he was weary, the little pony set back his ears and galloped, Cu running alongside.

Ahead of them in the moor in the scattered moonlight, Donald saw a fairy mound just ahead and growing on it was a rowan tree. 'That's meant for us. We'll find some shelter with the Good Neighbours this night,' said Donald. 'They're right fond of Janet, and she leaves cream out every night for them. But we're not going inside.'

To the fury of the witches, a crowd of Good Neighbours rushed out of the hill and circled both the fairy mound and the tired travellers. They led the exhausted pony to grass, and they let him rest on the rowan tree's roots. Donald leant against the pony's warm back, while Cu lay over his master's feet and dried out his sodden fur.

There wasn't a sound from the travellers or the fairies: nobody spoke. The witches swirled and screamed with the winds outside the hill circle, as if they were outside an invisible bubble. Inside, the Good Neighbours, seeing Donald's crook of rowan wood, sent for their pipers and drummers. They danced through the night, merry and defiant, while the weary travellers dozed in the warmth.

Then just before dawn, a cock crowed and the hill was suddenly empty of Good Neighbours and merry music and screaming witches and blackthorn broomsticks and howling

winds. All that was left was the glow of the dawn in the east, and the haze in the cold air and the damp of the moor.

'That was a powerful blessing Janet made,' said Donald. He got back on the pony, and all of them, dry and warm and well rested, went on their way to find the sheep. But they never ever said a word of thanks, for they knew that the Good Neighbours don't like it.

STORY SOURCES AND
FURTHER READING

Balfour, M.C., *Legends of the Lincolnshire Cars* (Folk Lore Society, 1891)

Bevan-Jones, R., *The Ancient Yew: A History of* Taxus Baccata (Windgather Press, 2004)

Briggs, K., *A Dictionary of British Folk Tales* (Routledge and Kegan Paul, 1971)

Broome, D., *Fairy Tales from the Isle of Man* (Penguin, 1957)

Crossley-Holland, K., *British Folk Tales* (Orchard Books, 1987)

Edmonston, B., and Saxby, J. M. E., *The Home of a Naturalist* (J. Nisbet, 1888)

d'Este, S. and Rankine, D., *Visions of the Cailleach* (Avalonia, 2008)

Folkard, R., *Plant Lore, Legends, and Lyrics* (Lowe, Marston, Searle and Rivington, 1884)

Garner, A., *Book of British Fairy Tales* (Collins, 1984)

Hagender, F., *Yew: A History* (Sutton Publishing, 2007)

Hagender, F., *The Heritage of Trees: History, Culture and Symbolism* (Floris Books, 2001)

Hunt, R., *Popular Romances of the West of England* (1865)

Hutton, R., *The Stations of the Sun* (Oxford University Press, 1996)

Jacobs, J., *English Fairy Tales* (David Nutt, 1890)

Jacobs, J., *Celtic Fairy Tales* (David Nutt, 1892)

Keightley, T., *The Fairy Mythology* (1828)

Kerven, R., *Faeries, Elves and Goblins* (National Trust, 2013)

Killip, K., *St Bridget's Night: Stories from the Isle of Man* (Hamish Hamilton, 1975)

Mabey, R., *Flora Britannica* (Sinclair Stevenson, 1996)

Mac Coitir, N. *Ireland's Trees: Myths, Legends and Folklore* (The Collins Press, 2015)

Mac Coitir, N. *Ireland's Wild Plants: Myths, Legends and Folklore* (The Collins Press, 2015)

Mackenzie, D. A., *Wonder Tales from Scottish Myth and Legend* (Frederick A. Stokes & Co., New York, 1917)

Marwick, E.W., *The Folklore of Orkney and Shetland* (Birlinn, 1975)

Matthews, C., *Celtic Memories* (Barefoot Books, 2003)

Morrison, S. *Manx Fairy Tales* (David Nutt, 1911)

Paterson, J.M., *Tree Wisdom* (Thorsons, 1996)

Peacock, M., *Tales and Rhymes in the Lindsey Folk-Speech* (George Jackson & Son, 1886)

Rackham, O., *The History of the Countryside* (Orion Books, 1986)

Rhodes, M.B., *Songs and Stories of Ruth Tongue* (Halsway Manor Society, 2009)

Riordan, J., *Folk-tales of the British Isles* (Raduga, 1987)

Robinson, D.J., *Folklore I* (1890)

Rolleston, T.E., *Celtic Myths and Legends*, (T. Y. Crowel, New York, 1911)

Sharman, V.D., *Folk Tales of Devon* (Thomas Nelson & Sons, 1952)

Sikes, W. *British Goblins: Welsh Folk-lore, Fairy Mythology, Legends and Traditions* (1881)

Tanner, H. and R., *Woodland Plants* (Impact Books, 1981)

Thomas, W. J., *The Welsh Fairy Book* (Frederick A. Stokes, 1907)

Tongue, R., *Somerset Folklore* (The Folklore Society, 1965)

Tongue, R., *Forgotten Folk Tales of the English Counties* (Routledge & Kegan Paul, 1970)

Tongue, R. and Rhodes, M.B., *Songs and Stories of Ruth Tongue* (Halsway Manor Society, 2009)

Vickery, R., *Garlands, Conkers and Mother-die: British and Irish Plant-Lore* (Continuum, 2010)

Yates, D.E., *A Book of Gypsy Folk Tales* (Phoenix House, 1948)

Also from The History Press…

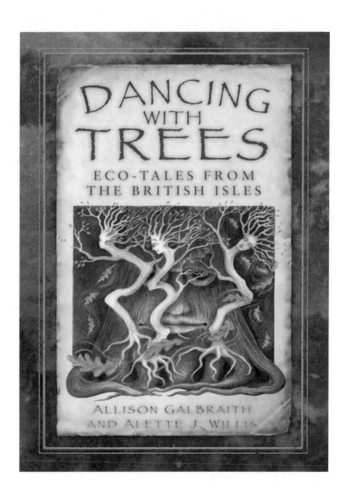

The oral storytelling traditions of the British Isles have connected people to the land and to their plant and animal neighbours for centuries. This collection brings together story wisdom from England, Scotland, Wales and Ireland that speaks to the heart of humanity's relationship with nature.

Whether it's traditional stories about native birds and animals or tales of living in harmony with the landscapes we call home, there's something here for everyone who believes that a more beautiful world is within our reach.

Richly illustrated with thirty original drawings, these enchanting folk tales will appeal to everyone interested in nature and in environmental conservation and will be enjoyed by readers, storytellers and listeners time and again.

WHERE
DRAGONS
SOAR

AND OTHER ANIMAL FOLK TALES
OF THE BRITISH ISLES

PETE CASTLE

Within these pages are tales of scheming creatures and ferocious animals from across the British Isles, passed down through the generations. Amongst the more famous beasts of myth and legend, such as the Loch Ness monster lurking in Scotland's black waters and the Hartlepool monkey that was mistaken for a French spy, are the less well-known stories of the peculiar, fantastical and extraordinary.

Discover the fox Scrapefoot and his run-in with bears, the fisherman's wife who was really a seal, and the two warring dragons hidden under Caernarf on – all brought to life by noted storyteller Pete Castle.

Illustrated with unique drawings, these enchanting tales will appeal to young and old, and can be enjoyed by readers time and again.

Society *for*
Storytelling

Since 1993, The Society for Storytelling has championed the ancient art of oral storytelling and its long and honourable history – not just as entertainment, but also in education, health, and inspiring and changing lives. Storytellers, enthusiasts and academics support and are supported by this registered charity to ensure the art is nurtured and developed throughout the UK.

Many activities of the Society are available to all, such as locating storytellers on the Society website, taking part in our annual National Storytelling Week at the start of every February, purchasing our quarterly magazine Storylines, or attending our Annual Gathering – a chance to revel in engaging performances, inspiring workshops, and the company of like-minded people.

You can also become a member of the Society to support the work we do. In return, you receive free access to Storylines, discounted tickets to the Annual Gathering and other storytelling events, the opportunity to join our mentorship scheme for new storytellers, and more. Among our great deals for members is a 30% discount off titles from The History Press.

For more information, including how to join, please visit

www.sfs.org.uk